LOVE ON MY LIST

LOVE ON MY LIST

by

Rosemary Friedman

Dales Large Print Books
Long Preston, North Yorkshire,
BD23 4ND, England.

British Library Cataloguing in Publication Data.

Friedman, Rosemary
Love on my list.

A catalogue record of this book is
available from the British Library

ISBN 1-84262-316-8 pbk

Published in Large Print 2004 by arrangement with
House of Stratus

Dales Large Print is an imprint of Library Magna Books Ltd.

Printed and bound in Great Britain by
T.J. (International) Ltd., Cornwall, PL28 8RW

To D.

One

After I had been in general practice for eighteen months and married for six, I began to realise that I had taken only the first halting steps on the path to becoming a good family doctor and that there was more to a harmonious marriage than remembering to put the lid back on the toothpaste.

If in my first year of caring for my now familiar patients I had acquired a bedside manner and a certain intuitive skill in looking after them, in my second I gained, in addition to one or two grey hairs, what I suppose can only be called compassion. To my routine visits and consultations, I found myself bringing a warmer heart and to the endless tales of woe, from the most minute psychological pinprick to the severest organic trauma, I lent a gentler ear.

Although the National Health Service had made the old-style family doctor, who lingered over a glass of sherry or a cup of tea with each patient, a practical impossibility, I felt that this essential figure of the last century should not be replaced by a 'pill-dispensing' automaton. There had, it was true, been dramatic advances in medicine over the past fifty years as there would undoubtedly be in the next, yet in an age when pimply youths thought nothing of beating up either each other or defenceless old ladies, I was convinced that there was still a need to minister to the family as a whole. The progress we have made in medicine may have given us control over many diseases of the body, yet it still has not eliminated the need to treat people with sympathy as well as pain with drugs.

As an established practitioner of eighteen months' standing, I now knew that the complaints I faced daily were not only the ones with names to be found in every morning paper and on the lips of every modern man.

Poliomyelitis, allergy, leukæmia, and operations on the brain and heart were acceptable small-talk in any gathering, but the diseases with which I had most commonly to deal would neither make interesting conversation nor sell any newspapers. Their names were Failure, Weariness, Misunderstanding and Discouragement, and they accounted for a large percentage of the patients who packed my surgeries. These were the chronic maladies of a generation with a background of blood-spattered years, facing a future made sombre with the general unrest of peoples and the specific fear of the hydrogen bomb. The family group, integrated and secure, of a century ago, had largely disappeared, and we were left with a wandering tribe of so-called 'independent' people who often sought, in middle life, for the security they had fought so hard to destroy in their youth. They lived in fear. Fear of not making enough money, fear of their social standing and, above all, fear of premature death from one of the much publicised fatal diseases. It was not now merely a question of keeping up with the Joneses; it was a matter of getting ahead while there was still time. Perhaps it was trespassing on the sphere of the priest to help these people go forth into the darkness, but the fact remained that they did not go to the priest. They came, morning and evening, to my surgery. It was impossible, in caring for my patients, not to learn to care about them.

Whether this change, obvious, or so I thought, only to my own perceptive soul-searchings, was the inevitable result of advancing maturity, or due to my newly married status, I don't know. My private opinion supported the view that whatever improved service I was giving my patients was due to the influence on my home and work of Sylvia, to whom at long last I was married.

It seemed so long ago that I had first proposed to her and had given up my hospital post for general practice in order to be able to support her, that she had turned me down and become engaged to the odious Wilfred Pankrest. The grisly thought that she had come so near to marrying that wealthy, knee-high-to-a-duck playboy whom she didn't love, made me shudder, but I preferred not to think about it. Sometimes I could hardly believe that she was actually my wife, and after six months I certainly hadn't got over the wonder of being married to her. I knew that I was a lucky man. I was happy in my practice, liked my work and my patients, and had a growing National Health list. Now I had love as well.

Poor Sylvia! Sometimes I felt pangs of conscience as I watched her cope manfully and simultaneously with a steak and kidney pie and a cryptic message from the laboratory, the proper spelling of which invariably eluded her, or found her, dripping wet from the bath, her teeth chattering with cold, as she listened to some time-consuming, rambling message from which she had ultimately to make a résumé.

As a top fashion model she had been used to long hours and hard work. For years now she had spent her days dashing from studio to smart hotel and Couture House to airport, when she wasn't standing for hours at a time before the camera; now the only places to which she dashed were the doors and the telephone, and the only apparatus before which she stood was the kitchen sink. True she had only exchanged one arduous task for another, but this time there was no applause.

I had, as well as I could, prepared her before our marriage for her rôle as the wife of a GP. It was no surprise to her, therefore, when she found that she was expected, with no training whatsoever, to operate a casualty clearing station, which entailed anything from dealing calmly with panic telephone calls while I was out on my rounds, to doing the odd emergency dressings which presented themselves at the waiting-room door out of surgery hours. She had anticipated many of her own duties as the wife of a GP and thought she knew a good deal about mine. What amazed her, though, about general practice was the way one could save a life between shaving and breakfast, regarding it almost as a matter of routine, or pronounce a man dead at lunch-time and come back calmly to eat one's soup. Knowing the misgivings she had had, which had kept her for over a year from marrying me, about her ability to settle down to life as the wife of a suburban GP, I watched her apprehensively as the first months slipped by. Whatever hazards, though, we had to overcome during our early married life were insignificant compared to the ghastly trials of the weeks before we actually reached the altar.

This pre-wedding period made jumping

beans out of nerves I never knew I had, and reduced my weight by half a stone. Had it gone on for much longer I doubt if I should have survived it.

There seemed to be endless weeks, before the date set for the wedding, of attempting to divide my attention fairly between carbuncles and cupboards (new fitted ones for the kitchen), and tonsils and various tones of grey (all of which looked the same to me) for the walls of the dining-room. During this time it often surprised me that I never answered 'pale blue everglaze' when asked by a patient what kind of elastic stockings she should wear, or recommended Mr Hicks, our plumber, when sending someone for a second opinion on what many of the patients referred to as their 'waterworks.'

Much to my surprise the Happy Day did eventually arrive and on it all went smoothly. Faraday, my colleague, best friend, and best man, remembered the ring, the rector a pretty speech with suitable references to my Honourable Profession and Noble Calling, and my mother not to shed more than one unobtrusive tear. By eleven o'clock, when I was normally walking down the garden path with my case to do the morning visits, I was marching slowly down the aisle with Sylvia.

The rest of the day I remember only as a hazy performance of handshakes, toasts, coy sentiment and ribald jokes in which Sylvia, indescribably beautiful in the white dress Michael Reed had created especially for her, was the star and my part so very insignificant that at times I wondered why I had come along. I did, however, provide the foil for her beauty, make a very short speech and give Sylvia's Uncle John something for his lumbago.

Our honeymoon was spent in the South of France and, apart from its more obvious delights, was memorable in that for two weeks I didn't see a single ill person and used the telephone only to order breakfast. We arrived home on a wet Wednesday, our heads full of happy memories of soft, ink-blue nights, lazy Pernods in the sun and the leisured life of the Côte d'Azure. It took us about two minutes to get the stars out of our eyes.

Faraday, who had been acting as my locum while he waited for his new hospital job to start, opened the door to us, kissed Sylvia soundly and nearly kissed me in his relief at seeing us.

'Busy?' I said, and picked up one of the suitcases which the taximan had dumped on the doorstep.

Faraday clapped a hand to his forehead. 'I'm going mad,' he said. 'Thank God you've come home.'

I started to step inside, but felt a tug at my elbow.

‘Haven’t you forgotten something?’ Sylvia said.

I cast an eye over the bags and cases.

‘I don’t think so, dear.’

Faraday whispered in my ear.

I put down the suitcase and picked up Sylvia. In the hall two pairs of eyes watched us incredulously. One belonged to a white-faced girl who was sitting on a battered suitcase, and the other to a smarmy-looking young man with shiny black hair.

Embarrassed by the audience, I looked round for somewhere to put Sylvia, who was waggling her legs in the air in an abandoned fashion. Since she was gazing into my eyes she hadn’t noticed that we had company. She pulled my head towards her and put her lips lovingly on mine.

Faraday cleared his throat and the reception committee looked tactfully at the ceiling. Chivalry, I decided, had had its due for the day. I set Sylvia firmly if unceremoniously on the floor and pulled her into the morning-room. Faraday followed us and we shut the door.

‘Now,’ I said, ‘perhaps you can put me in the picture. For a start maybe you could tell me who all these people are. You haven’t by any chance been taking in lodgers?’

Faraday lit a cigarette. I noticed that his hands were none too steady.

‘It’s quite simple. The girl is the maid you

ordered from the agency, and has just arrived from Ireland. The man just came a few minutes before you did and said he wanted to see you on a matter of the greatest importance. I've only just finished the surgery and I've twelve visits to do, so with your permission, old man, I'll be on my way. We'll have a chat later, and with the greatest pleasure in the world I'll hand you back the keys of your kingdom where no meal can be eaten in peace and in the service of which I shouldn't be at all surprised to have acquired a large peptic ulcer.'

Faraday made for the door, but came back to peer into my face.

'You're looking rather pale, old man,' he said. 'You don't want to overdo this marriage business, you know!'

He kissed Sylvia again and was off.

I delegated Sylvia to take the maid upstairs and deal with her, and called the young man into the morning-room.

'Now,' I said, taking an immediate dislike to his appearance; 'what can I do for you?'

He held out his hand. 'I'm Doctor Compton,' he said, 'Archibald Compton.'

We shook hands. 'Yes?'

He wandered over to the window, where the rain was streaming down the panes. 'It's very pleasant round here.'

'Extremely. Won't you sit down?'

'No. I can see I haven't called at a very

convenient time. I don't want to detain you.'

'What can I do for you?'

'Busy practice?' he said, swaying back and forth on his heels.

'Extremely.'

'Full list?'

A horrible suspicion began to enter my head. 'Doctor Compton,' I said, my manner less friendly. 'I hardly know you. These are very personal questions. Perhaps you'd better tell me why you called.'

He looked at his nails. 'I'm putting up a plate,' he said; 'I don't expect you'll be sorry to get rid of a few patients.'

I looked at him in horror. 'Squatting?'

'Horrible term,' he said. 'Putting my plate up.'

'Where?'

'Well, it's round the corner, actually. Number thirty-five.'

'Not the Johnsons' old house?' It was practically on my doorstep.

'That's right.'

I advanced menacingly. 'You can't do that,' I said. 'The Executive Council...'

He held up his hand. 'As a matter of fact,' he said, 'I've done it.'

Two

The maid was familiar with neither gas, electricity, running water nor flushing toilets. The Hoover terrified her, the cooker petrified her and when the telephone rang she crouched in a corner telling her beads. On the first day, having filled the sink with washing-up water for her, Sylvia came back half an hour later to find her bailing it out with a cup and throwing each cupful out of the window into the garden. When Sylvia demonstrated the miracle that occurred with the removal of the plug it quite made her day. She kept nipping surreptitiously to the sink, filling it with water and watching it disappear again.

It was a pity that Mrs Little, who had been my housekeeper since my first day in general practice, had given me her notice as soon as she heard of my marriage plans. But, as she said, she only liked to 'do' for single gentlemen and would never consider playing second fiddle in 'her' kitchen. Possibly it was all for the best anyway; I had always taken the line of least resistance, thankful that the house ran as smoothly as it did, but I doubt if some of Mrs Little's activities would have satisfied Sylvia's vigilant and fastidious eye. Anyway, Mrs Little had seen me safely married, given me a tea-cosy for a wedding present and departed to look after a gentleman in Balham. The gods, who in their divine wisdom look after the general practitioners, sent Bridget; I don't know what I had done to anger them.

Anyway, if Sylvia had her worries in the shape (peculiar as it was) of Bridget, a new husband and a new house to run, I also had mine.

My practice under the ministrations of Faraday had got a little out of control. He was used to seeing patients in hospital who had already been through the sieve of general practice and were in need of his specialised and prolonged attention. He had applied the same principles to my practice, with the result that he had usually not finished the morning surgery by lunch-time and the evening one by nine o'clock. It was hardly surprising that he considered me a grossly overworked slave of the State and returned, well satisfied, to his own less onerous if less remunerative job. On the patients, his methods had had varying effects. They were impressed by his kindness, his solicitude and the impression he gave that he had all the time in the world to spend with each one of them. They were not so impressed with his tendency to strip them and make a complete examination with the possible inclusion of a blood test, when they came to the surgery only for a 'pick-me-up,' the weekly bottle of medicine they had been having for years, or merely to read the magazines in the waiting-room and for a chat. Exhaustive examinations of the nervous system were run-of-the-mill for Faraday, but it was probably many years since he had opened an abscess or treated a case of measles. Neither was he in the habit of looking down ears, and one inflamed one which he had been treating daily with antibiotics cleared up immediately when I removed a piece of impacted cotton-wool from its depths.

To their utter confusion he made all my old men abandon their well-loved pipes and baccy ('the smoke helps me bring up the phlegm, Doctor') and lectured the young mothers soundly and firmly on giving no quarter to the family thumb-suckers. He had frightened them all so with his powerful personality and sense of the dramatic that they had all done as he said, but within a week of my return the pensioners were all once again sucking happily at their pipes and the children at their thumbs.

As I got into the swing of things again, getting the ropes back firmly into my own hands, I was flattered to see how much most of the patients depended on their 'own' particular doctor, rather than just any qualified person sitting at the surgery desk dispensing treatment and advice.

Faraday had seen a good many of my patients for me and had considered himself very busy, but I was surprised at the large number of people who had been saving up their complaints for my return. The excuses varied: 'You know my case, Doctor'; 'I reckoned he wouldn't know as much about arthritis (or boils or urticaria or catarrh) as you do'; or merely, 'I felt I couldn't talk to him like I can to you, Doctor.' It was nice to know it wasn't only the medicine, but the man, that mattered, and that there was a certain therapeutic value in the mere telling of the tale to the proper ear.

There was, of course, another side to the picture. Some of my patients came to see me, not for myself, but merely to 'the Doctor's.' They came because it was the house with the red light outside, probably the nearest to their homes, and here they knew they could get treated. Many of these people didn't even know my name. I was simply 'the Doctor.' To this minority it was of no importance whom they found behind the desk. Myself or Faraday; it made no difference. For all I knew an electrically propelled robot might have been acceptable provided he could wield convincingly a stethoscope and a pen.

Another section of the practice had actually welcomed my absence. There were some of the chronic sick, for whom there was no treatment except palliative, who had welcomed a new and sympathetic ear and the fresh display of interest in their symptoms provided by Faraday's thorough examination and attention to the weary history. He sent them home hugging their pathetic renewal of hope and a differently coloured bottle of medicine.

Others among the chronics merely grumbled that the 'other doctor' had altered the prescription they had been swallowing by the gallon for years and that they had in consequence taken a 'turn for the worse.'

Gradually I got things sorted out; relieved those who had waited of their burdens, dovetailed my own methods with the new treatments Faraday had meted out and pacified the chronics. As I did so I became more aware than before what an intuitive thing was general practice.

Now that the number of patients on my list had increased considerably, it was a practical impossibility to carry out a complete and exhaustive physical examination for every sniffle and itch that presented itself in the surgery; particularly when I had twenty to thirty patients to deal with in an hour and a half. This intuition, or possibly sixth sense, was an attribute not easily defined, but one indispensable to any Health Service practitioner to whom the only way to a comfortable living was a list with too many patients on it.

In treating most conditions the methods were clear-cut. A full examination was either patently necessary or not. It was in dealing with the small proportion of borderline cases that this – clairvoyance almost – was of supreme importance. Sometimes it was something in the way the patient described his symptoms to me that made me stop my pen on its way to prescribing a panacea and indicate the examination couch; very often there was nothing at all that I was conscious of that made me prescribe pastilles to suck for six sore throats and refer the seventh for a laryngoscopy to an ear, nose and throat surgeon, whose findings sometimes confirmed my suspicions.

This intuition had always stood me in good stead when the telephone rang in the middle of the night. That, however, was before I was married.

We had been home from our honeymoon for only a few weeks when the phone rang at two o'clock one morning. Sylvia, unused to this rude awakening, screamed and clutched my back. Tearing myself out of her grasp, I picked up the receiver.

'Is that the doctor?'

Grunt.

'This is Mr Meadows.'

Silence.

'Can you come over straight away, Doctor? My wife's feeling queer.'

'Tell me her symptoms.'

'She can't breathe properly and she's got palpitations. She thinks she's going to die.'

Pause.

'What did you say, Doctor?'

'I didn't say anything; I was thinking. Mr Meadows of Nuttall Drive?'

'That's right.'

'Has she any pains anywhere?'

There was a whispered consultation at the other end of the phone.

'No, no pains anywhere, Doctor.'

I thought of Mrs Meadows – a strapping woman, menopausal, and often nervous about herself. This in itself did not mean there was nothing wrong with her, but the symptoms her husband had described did not add up to anything.

'Mr Meadows,' I said; 'you tell your wife that there's nothing the matter with her. She's not dying and the palpitations will soon pass. Give her a warm drink of milk and one of her pink sleeping tablets. If you're worried about her in the morning give me a ring.'

When I was back again under the covers Sylvia said: 'How do you know there's nothing the matter with her?'

'It just doesn't sound like anything.'

'You mean you just don't want to get out of bed.'

'Don't be ridiculous.'

'I used to think doctors were selfless.'

'Go to sleep,' I said, 'and let me worry about the patients.'

There was silence for a few moments. Normally I would have been fast asleep again, but I was wide awake thinking about Mrs Meadows lying breathless on her bed when Sylvia said:

'Suppose she dies and you didn't go.'

It was a statement rather than a question. I didn't reply and tried to settle to sleep.

Ten minutes later I was groping for my trousers.

'I'm glad you're going,' Sylvia said, and snuggled under the bedclothes.

When I got back it was nearly three o'clock. The light was on in the kitchen and my first thought was that I had surprised burglars. I closed the front door quietly, picked up my number five iron from my golf bag in the hall and crept towards the intruder. I flung open the kitchen door and found Bridget, fully dressed, her hair in curlers, making toast.

'Holymitherogod!' she gasped, crossing herself. 'What do you be doing, Doctor?'

Her eyes were glued to my person, and I suppose I must have presented an odd spectacle with my pyjama legs peeping from beneath my trousers, a ferocious look on my face and a golf club in my hand.

'Never mind me,' I said. 'What do you be doing making toast at this hour? Do you know what time it is?'

'I heerd yourself get up,' she said, the toast starting to catch, 'and thought you'd be wanting your breakfast.'

I switched off the gas, sent Bridget back to bed and crept upstairs, the horrid smell of burnt toast in my nostrils.

I took my things off and got into bed without putting the light on, and making less noise than a mouse. I did not want to wake Sylvia. When I had settled myself on my pillows she said: 'Well?'

'You might have told me you were awake.'

'You didn't ask me.'

' "Well" what, anyway?'

'What about Mrs Meadows?'

'Nothing the matter with her. They were both sitting in the kitchen drinking tea and eating Marie biscuits. They were most surprised to see me. Perhaps in future you'll allow me to deal with patients in my own way.'

Sylvia put her arms round me and warmed my freezing body.

'Sorry, Sweetie,' she whispered.

I grunted ungratefully, but after a few moments responded to her embrace and slept like a log until the unsavoury-looking Bridget placed a cup of stone-cold, beer-like tea by my bed and hurled the newspapers on to my chest.

Before I was married the aftermath of a night call had been entirely my own affair. I was short with the patients in my morning surgery, never talking when a grunt would do, rude to my housekeeper who neither cared nor noticed, and I frequently forgot to shave. Now the lack of sleep resulted in my first row with my wife, and I discovered that as far as marriage was concerned I had much to learn.

It started badly and with my socks. They were the lovat-green ones I always wore with my tweed suit, and they had a hole in them.

'Mrs Little always used to *mend* my socks,' I said as I hurled them across the dressing-table where Sylvia was doing her face.

'You've plenty more in the drawer.' She was dabbing at herself with a tissue.

'Not green ones.'

'Wear grey ones, then. Nobody looks at your socks.'

'That's not the point. Why can't you mend them?'

'Nobody should have holes in their socks when they've only been married a month. Anyway, with answering the phone and feeding you every five minutes during the day and looking after that stupid Bridget I haven't exactly had much time.'

'You married me,' I said nastily; 'you knew what it was all about, so don't grumble.'

'Who's grumbling?' She brushed her hair.

'You are.'

'I'm not, Sweetie. I'm merely explaining why I haven't mended your green socks.'

The battle of the socks was followed by a frigid silence at the breakfast table and a contest of wills as the telephone rang and, on principle, neither of us would get up to answer it.

'It's the duty of the doctor's wife to protect him from the patients,' I growled after the incessant peal had gone on for about three minutes and was giving me a headache. 'If I answer it I shall only be rude.'

'Then they'll see you in your true light,' Sylvia said, and went on eating her toast. 'I don't get appreciated, so I don't see why I should answer the phone because you're too lazy to get up.'

The ringing stopped and we waited expectantly for it to start again. Nothing happened. An hour later, when the calls for the day appeared to be non-existent we discovered that Bridget, fed up with the noise, had bravely taken the receiver off and laid it neatly by the side of the telephone.

Having begun badly, the day did not improve. My plaster scissors were not on my dressings trolley when I needed them but in the kitchen where Sylvia had been cutting Turkish towelling to make rollers, and I had asked a mother to bring her child for vaccination to the surgery and had forgotten to get the vaccine.

By lunch-time the atmosphere had not improved. We ate almost in silence, and feeling at my lowest ebb I decided to sleep for half an hour before I did the afternoon visits. This, however, was not to be.

I was just finishing my pudding when through the window I saw Ted Jenkins, a long-distance lorry driver, stop his ten-ton truck outside the house and hurl himself down the garden path.

'It's the missus, Doc,' he rasped as I opened the front door. 'I jus' come in for me dinner and she's sitting in the kitchen bleeding to death. It's all over the place.' His face was ashen.

'All right, Ted,' I said, 'I'll come straight away. Where does the blood seem to be coming from?'

'Looks like one o' them veryclose veins,' he said. 'She said she knocked it on the dustbin. I bin meanin' to git a noo one on account of the jagged me'al only I never got round to it, see, what wiv' the twelve an' a tanner a week on the telly...'

He saw me make for my car.

''Op in the lorry, Doc,' he said; 'I'll take yer.'

'All right. Just let me get my case.'

High up in the cockpit of the lorry I shut my eyes as Ted Jenkins manoeuvred the heavy vehicle round the narrow bends and over the unmade roads as though it was a dodgem car.

It was hardly surprising that Ted had been alarmed at what he saw in the kitchen when he had come home for his dinner. There was blood everywhere, pooling on the floor and making a gory spectacle of poor Mrs Jenkins who, pale with shock, was clutching her leg and muttering to the effect that she was losing her 'life's blood.'

She had indeed ruptured a varicose vein, but the situation was not as bad as it looked. Raising the bleeding leg high in the air I got the shaking Ted, who looked nearly as pale as his wife, to hold it there until the vein emptied and the bleeding stopped. While he did this I reassured them both that the patient was nowhere near dying and that blood always looked more than it actually was. To prove it I took some rags from under the sink and mopped some of it up. By the time the leg had stopped bleeding and I had cleared up most of the mess, Ted and his wife were looking a little better.

I strapped the leg, sent Mrs Jenkins up to lie on her bed and told Ted to make her some tea.

When she had gone, Ted, his hands still

shaking as he lit the gas, said, 'Fanks, Doc. I fought she was a gonner. Didn't half gimme a turn. Don't want to lose 'er yet, Doc. Not the old trouble an' strife.'

I had to smile at Ted's concern over his 'missus.' It was common knowledge that he had a girl in every long-distance port of call and that when he was at home he and Mrs Jenkins did nothing but brawl, to the varied disgust or amusement of the neighbours.

''Course I don't say she don't drive me clean round the bend at times with 'er nag, nag, nag, but I wouldn't want nuffink to 'appen to 'er. We bin married twenty-five years, Christmas.'

'I don't know how she's put up with you for so long,' I said, trying to unstick the strapping from where it had wound itself round my case.

'Ah!' Ted said. 'You gotta know 'ow to treat 'em.'

'I suppose you have,' I agreed, thinking of my morning words with Sylvia.

'They're all of a piece, wimmin,' Ted said from the depths of his vast experience. 'You gotta show appreshiashun.' He warmed the teapot expertly and enlarged upon his theme. 'It's like this, see. She gives you a steak an' kidney pud, fer yer tea. Hard as nails. Well, it's no good you saying you can't get yer bloomin' teef into it, 'cos she'll blow 'er top about not never knowing when you're comin' in, and stoppin' away nights, and Gawd knows what. You gotta swaller it, see. Tell 'er, 'That's a nice piece o' pastry, Marj an' nex' time she'll try 'arder 'cos she likes yer to say it's nice, see.'

'I see,' I said. 'That's how it's done, is it?'

He turned off the gas with a plop.

'Can't tell me nuffink abaht wimmin,' he said, 'not Ted Jenkins. Cuppa?'

'No thanks, Ted,' I said; 'I must be off. Give your wife her tea and tell her to come and see me in the surgery tomorrow. Then you'd better run me home.'

Back in my own house I was already feeling less sleepy and I decided to finish the rest of my visits straight away. All the afternoon Ted Jenkins' words kept sounding in my head: 'You gotta show appreshiashun!' I wondered if perhaps he was right.

As I came down the garden path after removing the stitches from little Jenny Hicks' abdominal wound following her appendicectomy, I noticed a large new, shiny black Allard parked outside the house next door, its snub nose looking disdainfully down the street. Out of it, carrying his case, stepped the smarmy Doctor Archibald Compton. I would have ignored him completely had it not been for the fact that people at the house he was going into were my patients. I asked him what he thought he was doing. He said he had been called to see a young lady who was staying with them. Sceptical, I resolved to investigate, and left him, raising his ridiculous bowler hat.

Sitting in my ancient little car, which had served me faithfully and which I had loved for many years, looking at the gleaming behind of the Allard, it occurred to me that if battle were to be done with Archibald Compton I must arm myself with efficient weapons. There was no doubt that my car was not only that of a nobody but was liable to fall to pieces at any time. I would have to consider in the very near future a model more worthy of a successful GP.

By four o'clock, my mood, engendered by the lack of sleep, had completely passed. I felt my old self again, and as I drove towards the house I looked forward to apologising to Sylvia for my churlishness, and perhaps taking some of Ted Jenkins' advice.

As I opened the front door I heard the high-pitched busy melody of female voices all talking at once. I put my head round the morning-room door and stopped dead. There were three elegant young women with Sylvia; each of whom regarded me with their 'doe-eyes' as if I were a piece of cheese. There was tea on the table and delicate-looking little cakes. Nobody offered me anything. Sylvia said: 'No more calls, dear,' her voice heavy with meaning, and I gathered that I was 'de trop.' They waited politely until I shut the door before they started their girlish squeaking again.

It was cold and deserted in the drawing-room, Bridget was in the kitchen, and I could not very well go and lie on my bed at four o'clock in the afternoon. Feeling fed up, I got into the car again and went down to 'Della's, Iced Cakes a Speciality,' for a cup of tea.

Three

By bed-time I was still annoyed at having had to go out for tea, and all my good resolutions had faded away.

'It must look very strange,' I said to Sylvia as we were getting undressed, 'for all the patients to see me having tea at "Della's, Iced Cakes a Speciality," when they know I've a perfectly good wife at home. I can't think why you have to ask all those twittering females for tea.'

'Sweetie, they are my friends,' Sylvia said. 'I must have some life of my own. You absolutely embarrassed the girls.'

'Embarrassed the girls!' I snorted. 'Whose house is this? You forget this is a place of business.'

'How can I forget it?' Sylvia's voice was rising. 'The phone, the door; I haven't had a decent bath since we've lived here because that nitwit of a maid can't answer the phone. She won't even hand out the prescriptions at the door; she just giggles and runs away. The only time I get out is when Miss Hornby comes, and that's only two hours, twice a week; then you complain just because I have a few friends to tea. I don't want to become an entire recluse, you know.'

I opened my mouth to say I knew it was all a mistake. She should never have given up modelling to marry me. That it was obviously no life for her and that she would never settle to it. Then I remembered Ted Jenkins and his philosophy of 'appreshiashun.'

'I know,' I said, studiously straightening out my tie, 'it's been pretty rotten for you, darling. I do think you've managed marvellously so far, considering you've never either run a house or coped with a patient before. The patients all think you're awfully sweet.'

Sylvia, one stocking on and one stocking off, looked at me incredulously.

I plunged on. 'Seriously. They say how kind you sound on the telephone, and helpful when I'm out. They get short shrift from most doctors' wives, I can tell you.'

She said nothing, regarding me as if I were a little mad. I decided to give the Jenkins technique one more chance, and after that tell her what I thought about her making me look an ass in my own home.

'And the meals,' I said. 'If I'd known you were such a good cook I would have forced you to marry me long ago. To think of the times I put up with Mrs Little's mince, shepherd's pies and blancmange.' I hung my tie on the rack and looked surreptitiously over my shoulder. She was coming towards me dangling her stocking.

'Do you really think I'm managing?'

'Superbly.'

'What about the girls to tea?'

'You're entitled to some relaxation.'

'We should have given you a cup of tea. I was upset because you'd been shouting at me all day.'

'I'm sorry. I'm always irritable when I don't get enough sleep. You mustn't take any notice.'

'I made you go out in the night for nothing.'

'You couldn't help it. I was overzealous myself in the beginning.'

Her arms were round my neck.

'Will I ever make a doctor's wife?'

'You have, angel.'

'Kiss me,' she said softly. 'But first tell me the incubation period for measles so that next time they ring up and ask I shan't have to bother you.'

'Eleven to fourteen days.' Her lips were very close.

'And is athlete's foot infectious?'

'There's a time and place for everything,' I said, holding her tightly to me.

We did not discuss athlete's foot again that night.

We decided that Bridget was untrainable and must go, and that Miss Hornby, my secretary, was to come for one whole day a week so that Sylvia could go out and enjoy herself sitting under various instruments of torture in the hairdresser's. I silently thanked Ted Jenkins for seeing me safely over the first hurdle in the marriage stakes. Things begun to run more smoothly.

When I had first given up the idea of taking my Membership of the Royal College of Physicians and had decided to go into general practice, I had resolved never to let myself decline into the family doctor who, from the time he set foot in his practice to his death or retirement some fifty years later, never read a medical journal or attempted to keep himself up to date. There was always much talk about the declining status of the GP under the National Health Scheme. To keep the family doctor at his former, respected level three things were essential: the trust of his patients, the respect of his colleagues, and the means to do his job adequately. This last point seemed to me most important. Neglect in keeping up to date with recent medical advances could only lead to doing a second-best job. Apart from being unfair to the patients under one's care, this had never appealed to me. It never amused me when patients said of the old doctor, my predecessor, 'He always said, "Do what you think best, Mrs Simpkins," when I asked him about feeding problems. "I always think a mother knows more than the doctor when it comes to feeding a baby."' Perhaps in nine cases out of ten he had been right. But the tenth case might have turned out better if he had taken the trouble to study the problems of infant feeding and keep up to date with the recent advances in pædiatrics. He managed to gloss over his ignorance by flattering the mother. It was both lazy and dishonest.

There were not only good medical journals published every week describing any new medical advances and discussions, but also free refresher courses available to general practitioners and held in various parts of the country. Since these courses were always popular and heavily booked (particularly when held in the vicinity of good golf courses) I had reserved a place the year before for a course in General Medicine which was to be held in Edinburgh in two months' time.

I hated the idea of leaving Sylvia after we had been married such a short time, and was not too happy about leaving the patients again so soon after I had had time off for my honeymoon. Sylvia and I discussed the problem at length, and came to the conclusion that it would be in the ultimate interest of the patients if I went on the course and that, much as I disliked leaving her and she to be left alone, we should both survive. It was, after all, for two weeks only, and we could write and phone each other every day. Perhaps what we dreaded most were the lonely nights, but we tried to console each other that it was all in a good cause.

That problem having been decided, the next step was to obtain the services of a locum. I rang the British Medical Association and put my name down on their lists.

In the surgery I kept a vigilant eye open for my patients who were in the motor-car trade and told them of my requirements. First of all I was interested in a car that was reliable; the starter must respond when I tottered to the garage on the coldest night; it must have a good heater, a windscreen defroster that worked, electric wipers, with water squirt to remove mud, first-class headlamps – not both on the same fuse – and a real fog lamp. It must turn in the road like a taxi and have effortless steering, but not so low-geared that it took five turns of the wheel from lock to lock. It must be draughtproof, both exit and entry being easy for non-contortionists, and, since its owner was one notoriously careless with morphine and phenobarbitone (usually under the seat in my present car) it must all lock securely. These requirements were most probably inherent in any new car, but since I was used to driving round in a leaking, spluttering, rattling, rusting, wiperless box on wheels for so long I felt it necessary to be explicit about my needs. In addition, the said car was to be moderately priced, dignified and by comparison make that of Doctor Archibald Compton slink from the road in embarrassment. Each and every dealer I spoke to assured me they had the Very Thing.

One morning one of my visits was to the house which I had seen Doctor Archibald Compton leaving the week before. Mrs Warrington and her family had been good patients of mine and I came straight to the point: I wanted to know what had been going on.

'As a matter of fact, Doctor,' she said, 'he came to see our new maid. Apparently Doctor Compton is a specialist on skins, and it was a rash that was bothering her. I told her that you were our doctor, but she said that her friend swears by Doctor Compton, so she gave me the little card and I rang him up for her. Her English isn't very good, particularly on the telephone.'

'Little card?' I said. 'What little card?'

Mrs Warrington led the way up the stairs to where Angela, whose sore throat I had come to see, was ill.

'Oh! just one of those little visiting cards; you know, with his telephone number on it. Please don't think it was my fault, Doctor; you know I wouldn't have anyone for the children or myself except you.'

I could see she was getting upset about my harping on Doctor Archibald Compton. I examined little Angela, a nice seven-year-old with acute follicular tonsillitis, and heard all about the 'grilla' she had seen in the Zoo at half term, before I resumed the subject.

Giving Mrs Warrington the prescription for oral penicillin, I said casually:

'I suppose you couldn't find the little visiting card for me, could you?' She looked blank, her mind still on Angela.

'Doctor Compton's card; I wanted his phone number; he isn't in the book yet,' I said wildly.

'Of course, Doctor. I'll call Hildegarde.'

Hildegarde, after much 'Ja, Ja-ing,' said, 'Ja, I haf him in mein Zimmer,' and plodded teutonically off in her knitted stockings to get it.

As I thought, the 'specialist in skins' had no more qualifications than I. I slipped the card in my pocket. Advertising, in the eye of the General Medical Council, was no joke.

As I opened the front door with my key and stepped into the hall I heard Sylvia on the telephone in the kitchen.

'I'm sorry, but he's out,' I heard her say;

'but I'll tell you what to do. Sit him bolt upright – no, not lying down, Mrs Miffle – bolt upright, and press his nostril tightly the side where the bleeding is, for three minutes by the clock. Yes, I'm sure it will stop; but if it hasn't, ring up again in half an hour and I expect Doctor will be back. Not at all. Goodbye.' She put down the receiver and it was white with flour from the pastry she was making.

I put my arms round her and held her tightly. She was powerless because of her floury hands.

'And since when did you know how to stop a nosebleed?' I said.

'Remember Mr Boon in the middle of the night last week?'

'I thought you were asleep.'

'You thought wrong. Let me get this pie in the oven.' She struggled to get away.

I didn't release my grip.

'You did very well, darling. I'm proud of you.'

'There's nothing to it,' she said. 'I really don't know why you have to spend six years qualifying!'

'Any messages or anything?' I picked a cherry out of the pie she was putting together.

'Only Faraday to invite himself to dinner; and I've got what sounds the most wonderful maid coming to see me this afternoon.

Oh yes! And somebody brought you a little gift. I put it on your lunch place. I was dying to open it but I didn't.'

Curious and somewhat suspicious about my present, I went into the dining-room and removed the package, wrapped in layers of tissue paper and tied with pink string, from my side plate. I undid it and my suspicions were confirmed.

In the kitchen Sylvia glanced round from the oven as I held it aloft.

'Goody! A bottle,' she said. 'Is it sherry or whisky? We need both, anyway.'

'It's a specimen,' I explained, 'somebody's urine. It's always best to take anything handed in at the door straight into the surgery. Except perhaps at Christmas time.'

The pie safely in the oven, Sylvia straightened up, flushed from the heat.

'Oh, Sweetie!' she said. 'Aren't I an idiot?'

'No damage done. How could you possibly know? They're always too embarrassed to say what's in the parcel.'

Sylvia giggled. 'You should have heard me thanking him. I thought he gave me rather an odd look when I said, "Thank you very much indeed. How kind of you. I'm sure Doctor will ring you up and thank you personally."'

'Never mind, darling. You did stop the nosebleed. I think I'll just take this specimen down to the Path. Lab. before lunch. I want to get it analysed quickly, if possible.'

Outside the Path. Lab. I recognised the snooty face of the shiny black Allard.

Doctor Compton was talking to my favourite, red-haired technician as I walked in with my bottle. I ignored him completely and gave her my most appealing smile.

'I wonder if Doctor Benson could spare a few moments to spin this down for me and let me know if there are any pus cells,' I said.

She smiled back. 'I'm so sorry, Doctor. Doctor Benson is busy just now doing a blood count for Doctor Compton, and after that he has twenty cultures to do. It won't be till late afternoon, I'm afraid. If you'll just fill the form in and leave it with me and he'll see to it as soon as possible.'

Filling in my yellow form, I felt Archibald Compton smirking behind my back and trying to impress my red-haired friend. Turning round I caught her bestowing the same flashing smile upon him as she always did upon me. She went down immediately in my estimation.

By the time I had completed my form, Doctor Compton's blood count was ready and we had no choice but to walk down the long, dark, narrow corridor together.

'Nice girl, that ginger one,' he said chattily. 'She was telling me she comes from Southport. She's getting married next month to one of the orthopædic chaps. They've been engaged for two years.'

Chagrined, I could think of nothing to say. He had found out more about her in his month in practice than I had in a year.

As we came out into the bright daylight my fingers closed around the little card in my pocket. I brought it out and thrust it under his nose.

'I see it pays to advertise,' I said.

'Where did you get that?'

'From that German maid you went to see.'

He laughed easily. 'Oh! She's a friend of my housekeeper's. I gave it to Ilse when she went to register with the police so that she'd get the name and address right. I suppose she passed it on to this other girl.' He held out his hand for it.

I slipped it into my pocket. 'I'd like to keep it, if you don't mind. You never know when I might need a "skin specialist?"'

He shrugged, but had the grace to blush as he got into his car. I felt that I had more than paid him back for his success with Ginger in the Path. Lab. and for getting to Doctor Benson first with his blood count.

While I was still pulling at the starter and my engine was spluttering and dying with a dismal whine, he zoomed past me with a boom-boom-boom of eight cylinders and a condescending wave of his yellow-gloved hand.

I wasn't so sure that I'd had the last word after all.

Four

Mv morning post a week later was, as usual, interesting. It was always prolific, and I often annoyed Sylvia by selecting the more lurid items from the daily pile of advertisements from the drug houses and laying them on her plate. She was often greeted, on sitting down at the breakfast table, with a highly coloured, glossy diagram of the lower bowel and the stark-lettered query 'CONSTIPATED?' Other equally horrid reproductions showed pictures of haggard men (stomach ulcers), pregnant women (anæmia), irritable children (worms), and fretful babies (inadequate artificial feeding). At times the advertisements took the form of calendars, pseudo-personal letters and tolerably pleasing reproductions of Old Masters; at others there was merely a single, bloodshot eye, the nasty fungicidal growth between two grossly enlarged, knobbly toes or simply a scaly, eczematous lip. In either case Sylvia was unimpressed, and we had now been married long enough for her to toss the morning's offering on the floor without comment. Her stomach was becoming stronger and she was well on the way to becoming a seasoned doctor's wife to whom pathological horrors were a necessary adjunct to breakfast, lunch and dinner.

This morning I found a picturesque rodent ulcer for Sylvia, put aside the rest of the advertisements in their large buff envelopes, and opened my first letter with a threepenny stamp, which was from Faraday, typed on his hospital notepaper, about a patient I had referred to him for his opinion. He thanked me formally for sending him the patient, summarised his findings, and ended '...his liver and spleen were not palpable and Hess' test was negative. I must therefore congratulate you on your diagnosis and agree with you that this man is suffering from some form of purpura, presumably, as you say, Henoch-Schoenlein in variety.'

Having signed the letter in his official capacity, he added the PS: 'So glad that marriage has not affected your diagnostic skill. Many thanks for the charming dinner and evening with you and Sylvia. Have felt lonely and jealous ever since. Ask Sylvia if she can find me a wife, preferably eighteen, innocent, 36-22-36 or near as poss. I leave the colour to you. PPS: There *was* albumen in his urine!'

I wondered if his hospital had a full copy of the letter, and handed it to Sylvia so that she could deal with his request.

There was a note from the BMA informing me that at the moment they had very few locums on their books for the period I had mentioned, since there was a large demand for them at present, but they had written to a Doctor O'Brien, who had applied to them, and he would be contacting me in about a week.

The next few letters were from various hospitals concerning patients, and the last was addressed to me on a pale blue envelope in a semiliterate, backward-sloping, hand. Sylvia looked at it curiously.

'Who's that from?'

'I don't know. I haven't opened it yet.'

Taking it out of my hand and examining it, she said: 'It's from a woman and it smells of scent. Cheap scent. Your past is catching up with you. Can I open it, Sweetie?'

'If you wish.'

I drank my coffee while Sylvia's eyes grew wider. Once as she read she said: 'Sweetie!' in amazement. Then, 'Sweetie, really!' Finally: 'Well, who's Renee Trotter?'

'Haven't a clue.'

'Really? She says she's "Yours always"! She also says, "God Bless" and "sleep well"!'

I held out my hand for the letter.

MY DEAREST BROWN EYES, *I read, and looked again at the envelope to make sure it was addressed to me*, or should I say Doctor? You will probably put on a superior air and say 'Poor Girl,' 'Woman,' whatever you wish to call me, 'is slightly worse for wear.' One way

I am. Anyway, how are you? I am very worried about you, darling. Working too hard, handsome one.

Seeing my Medico going round each day gives me moral support, if you get what I mean. When I awake from my slumbers I worry, do they know about us? Do not write to this address, you will understand why.

This is all for now,
Love to you my very dear,
God Bless, Sleep well,

Yours always,
RENEE TROTTER.

PS How is your wife?

'The girl's nutty,' I said.

Sylvia laughed. 'I believe you, Sweetie. How long has this been going on?'

'I couldn't say. I think I've only seen her once in the surgery. I can't even remember what she looks like.'

'What are you going to do about it?'

'Nothing.'

'Does this sort of thing happen often?'

I stood up and kissed the back of her neck. It was time to start the surgery. 'Frequently,' I said. 'That's what you have to put up with if you marry a "handsome Medico." 'Bye for now.'

'Cheerio, "dearest Brown Eyes,"' Sylvia said, and went to fetch the wastepaper basket from behind the curtain so that she could clear away some of the rubbish I had left on the breakfast table.

'Hey!' she shouted suddenly.

I came back into the room. 'What is it, Sweetie? I'm late.'

'You must have some wealthy patients.'

I joined her by the window. Outside the surgery entrance, together with the usual assortment of small cars, motorcycles, bicycles and prams, were three opulent-looking cars: a pale blue American convertible which looked about half a mile long, a bottle-green snazzy-looking MG and a gentlemanly black Rover.

They looked most impressive, and I wished I had taken the trouble to put on a stiff white collar.

The surgery was busy one. Ten minutes were taken up by arguing with Mrs Rumbold. We had been spoiling for a row for a long time and I wondered that it hadn't come before.

While approving in general principle of the National Health Service, its administration very often proved a tricky and time-consuming matter. I usually tried to find a happy medium in dealing with the countless demands made upon me; to keep the patients happy without incurring unnecessarily heavy charges on the Health Service. Sometimes, however, this was not so easy, and I often felt myself a kind of Roman dictator seeking popularity by distributing free corn to the masses; only in my case it was not corn I was doling out, but free sleeping pills, slimming pills, cough cures, cold cures, nerve tonics, 'pick-me-ups,' notes for work, notes for school, notes for coal, sunray lamps, corporation houses and corsets.

On the whole I found the patients co-operative when I tactfully chided them about excessive demands. Not so Mrs Rumbold.

She was a real 'moaner.' She disregarded the fact that I had during the past year saved her from premature death by my prompt diagnosis of her perforated ulcer, cured one of her children of bed-wetting, cared for her ailing husband, and seen one or other member of her family at least twice a week. Nothing I did, though, was ever good enough. The medicine usually 'made it worse,' no matter what 'it' was; the pills 'upset her stomach,' and nothing got better as quickly as she would like. Her husband's certificates were frequently wrongly dated, the chemist accused of giving her the 'wrong' prescription, and there were always too many people in the waiting-room. When I visited her to see the baby he had always just gone to sleep and she didn't like to disturb him; when she visited me she was surprised that I was unable to make a diagnosis without asking her to undress. She considered it a personal affront that I could not listen to her chest if she undid only one button of her cardigan. In one year she had had, in exchange for her contributions to the Health Service, more visits, operations, dressings, pills, placebos and 'tonics' than I cared to remember. Now she demanded iron tablets. I refused to give them to her.

'I think they'd do me good,' she said, pulling on her neat kid gloves. 'Doctor Compton gave them to my friend when she was feeling run-down and they've bucked her up enormously.'

'Perhaps your friend needed iron tablets, Mrs Rumbold,' I said. 'You had a blood test only a few weeks ago when you complained of feeling giddy, and you're not the slightest bit anæmic. I see no necessity for prescribing them for you.'

She pushed her face, with its sharp nose and thin lips, nearer to mine.

'They *are* available on the Scheme, aren't they?' she said threateningly.

'At my discretion.'

'I tell you I need them, Doctor. I'm utterly exhausted.'

I stood up. 'They'll do you no good at all, Mrs Rumbold, and I refuse to prescribe them for you. You cannot make your own diagnoses and expect me to prescribe for them. I'm the doctor, not you.'

'Well!' she said, standing up and quivering

with indignation. 'You've never done *me* the slightest good. I shall make a complaint to the Health Service. I shall change to my friend's doctor. He's a *Harley Street* man.'

'Doctor Compton is welcome to you,' I said rudely, fed up with Mrs Rumbold. It was a pity that I had to yield seven National Health cards to my competitor, but he was more than welcome to Mrs Rumbold.

She swept imperiously past me and out of the surgery. Her exit would have been dignified had she not carried with her my stethoscope dangling from one of the spokes of her umbrella. The next patient brought it back.

By ten-thirty the waiting-room was practically empty, and I still had seen nobody who looked as if they had stepped out of a lengthy convertible, a swish MG or a substantial Rover. Curious, I opened the waiting-room door to see who was left.

Mr Thwaite of 'Regent Motors,' Mr Ironside, manager of the local 'Blue Star' Garage, and George Leech from the kerb in Warren Street, sat glaring at each other through the smokescreen they had put up.

Together, without removing their hands from the pockets of their overcoats or their cigarettes from their mouths, they each assured me that in answer to the feeler I had put out for a new car, they had brought along the most dignified (Mr Thwaite, for his Rover), the nippiest (Mr Ironside, the MG), the smartest (George Leech of his convertible) car on the road.

I had an interesting and unusual morning. I visited a chicken-pox and a mastitis in the Rover, and an emphysema and a glandular fever in the MG. By the time I arrived at the largest and 'most desirable' residence in the district in the convertible with the top down, my head was spinning with details of compression ratios, cooling systems, turning circles, fuel consumption, dipped beams, recirculatory ball steering boxes and twin windtone horns.

Horace H Brindley was one of the wealthiest men in the neighbourhood. He was also my one and only private patient. At one time plain Bert Brindley from the provinces, he had had the good fortune to have his bicycle repair shop in the dead centre of a block of property where one of the big multiples was planning to erect a store. Aided and abetted by the friend who had lent him the money to set himself up in business and by his native shrewdness, inherited from a father who had managed to support himself and a family without ever working for more than two or three weeks at a stretch, he had firmly refused the first tempting offers dangled before his nose. They had actually started building round him before Bert Brindley decided the price was right, left the provinces, never to return, and gave birth to the H H Brindley Bicycle Company whose products were known and bought all over the world. 'HH,' as he now liked to be known, having received his initial shove, climbed steadily up the ladder. He married a wife, if not from the top drawer, from a good few drawers higher than his own, became known as a public benefactor, hung a Seurat and Manet on his walls, walked softly on Aubusson and settled down to a life of luxury. By the sheerest luck he had become my patient when he moved to the district a year ago.

His parlourmaid was the daughter of old Hodge, our gardener and odd-job man. It was she who had answered his shouts one morning when he had bent to pick up a newspaper and had been unable to straighten up again, and she who had telephoned for me. Pleased with my manipulation of his disc, he had asked me to continue to treat him and his family whenever necessary. I was delighted, especially when I had asked him for his medical cards and he had said: 'I've got plenty of brass, lad, and I don't want owt for nowt. You do take private patients, don't you?' I assured him that of course I did, although he and his family remained my sole cash customers.

This morning he was sitting up in bed leaning against the peach satin, quilted bedhead, smoking a six-inch cigar and reading the *Financial Times*, his glasses on the very end of his nose.

'It's me heart, lad,' he told me, pointing to his chest and putting his newspaper down on top of the *Daily Mirror*, 'and if there's owt wrong you'd better tell me.'

I took the history and examined him carefully, but could find nothing wrong. I reassured him and asked if he had anything on his mind.

'To be perfectly honest,' he said, getting out of bed and tying his pyjama trousers more tightly round his rotund abdomen, 'I have got something on me mind. I'm worried about our Tessa. She's a good lass but she's keeping the wrong company. I haven't given my daughter the best education money can buy to see her mixing with a bunch of lads with no brass and no brains. We take her to dances, her mother and me, the right dances, mind you, and for looks and clothes there's none can hold a candle to her, though I say it meself; but she comes along just to do us a favour. I told you she was a good lass, but it's as plain as the nose on your face she'd rather be out with her pals rocking and rolling all over the place. I know she's young and she needs her fun, not that I ever had much fun when I was young, but I'd like to see her moving in the right direction.'

He waved his hand round the bedroom,

large enough for a small ballroom, with its pearl-grey carpet, peach satin curtains and ormolu cherubs carrying everything from lights to flower vases. 'I'm not an unreasonable chap, but I haven't got where I have for nothing. She could have anyone, our Tessa could – and I mean anyone – I've got connections. And look what she does with herself!' He now had his crocodile slippers on and was fastening his black silk dressing-gown festooned with dragons and with 'HH' embroidered boldly in scarlet on the breast pocket. He added a white silk, self-patterned muffler and prowled round the bedroom with his hands in his pockets.

'I'd like her to marry someone with brains,' he said. 'Not "H H Brindley Bicycles" brains, but someone who knows what it's all about.'

He stopped prowling and stood stolidly before me. 'I've got twenty-five thousand pounds' worth of pictures hung on my walls,' he said, 'and I can't even spell names of chaps that painted them. There's ten yards of books in my bookcases, and I've never read one of them. I can't start learning about these things at my age, but I want someone with some appreciation of them for Tessa. She's been to Paris, to Switzerland and all over t' place being educated, and now she sits in coffee bars with a lot of brainless idiots!' he said bitterly. 'What am I to do with her?'

I shook my head. The problem of a husband for Tessa Brindley was outside my province.

'She went out with a medical man once, and Mother and me were quite excited when...' He went on abut the disappointing end to Tessa's romance with the medical man, but I wasn't listening. I had suddenly remembered Faraday and his request to us to find him a wife.

'I know a chap,' I said enthusiastically, but then I remembered. Faraday certainly knew a Manet from a Monet, but he hadn't two halfpennies for a penny. What use would he be to Tessa Brindley?

'Aye?'

'No,' I said, subsiding. 'It wouldn't do.'

Horace Brindley looked me in the eye. 'If it's a question of brass,' he said, 'I've got more than enough for Tessa. Don't worry on that score. What's he like?'

'A doctor,' I said, 'my oldest friend. Specialising in neurology. He's doing very well, but of course he hasn't yet got a consultantship. When he does...'

HH held up his hand. 'I can fix all that,' he said, 'if he's a good lad.'

'It doesn't work like that in medicine,' I said; 'it's not a question of money.'

'I've got friends as well,' he said; 'there's always strings that can be pulled. I'd have him in Harley Street in no time.'

I shuddered as I thought of what Faraday would say to this airy disposal of his academic aspirations, although Tessa Brindley, at eighteen, more than fulfilled his list of requirements, having one of the most beautiful figures and faces I had ever seen. She was also a charming girl.

HH slapped me on the back. 'Fix it up, lad,' he said; 'fix it up and I'll see you're all right.' He made me feel like a taxi driver, but I knew that in spite of his brashness he meant well.

I was a bit sorry I had opened my mouth about Faraday at all but, having done so, promised to arrange a meeting.

HH accompanied me to the door in his dressing-gown. I had to explain about the smart convertible which George Leech was dusting with his silk handkerchief, and I asked HH his opinion as to what make of car I should buy.

'It's not so much what *you* want, lad,' he said: 'what about your wife? It's no earthly use you getting a Rover if she fancies herself in an MG, or vicky-verky. They always have the last word, you know. I discovered that a long while back.'

Of course, he was right. I had quite forgotten that Sylvia might be interested in our new car, and wondered if I would ever learn all there was to know about marriage.

With his crocodile slippers crunching on the gravel of the well-kept drive HH beckoned me to follow him. We walked round to his garage and there, outside the huge triple doors, stood the most elegant Rolls-Royce, certainly the most expensive I had seen outside the Motor Show. He ran a hand over her lovingly.

'Now there's a car,' he said.

'I'd have one of those, of course,' I said, 'but I'm afraid it wouldn't go in my garage.'

HH looked at me shrewdly. 'You never know your luck, lad,' he said. 'You fix our Tessa up and anything could happen.'

Driving home beside George Leech, my mind on Rolls-Royces, Faraday, Tessa Brindley, Rovers and MGs, I listened with only one ear as he enthused lengthily about the appearance, performance and exceptional value of the convertible he was trying to sell me.

Outside the house I thanked him for his help and told him, as I had told Messrs Thwaite and Ironside, that unfortunately all the cars they had shown me that morning were too expensive, but that as soon as I had made up my mind about something more within my price range I would get in touch with him. In any case, I said, I would have to discuss the matter with my wife.

George Leech understood. 'Natch,' he said, sliding into the driving seat. 'Gotta keep 'em happy. Bless 'em.'

Everybody seemed to know how to treat a wife except me.

In my hurry to get out in my new cars I had forgotten to take my door key. I rang the bell. The door swung wide and holding it was a middle-aged woman with a deadpan face, dressed in a black dress with a frilly lilac-coloured cap and apron. For a moment I wondered if I had come to the right house; then I remembered it was Monday – the day that Bridget was going and the new maid arriving.

'Aim so sorry,' the vision said, unsmiling: 'Doctor's out.'

'That's all right,' I said, 'I am the doctor. How do you do?'

'Oh!' she said. 'Aim so sorry, sir,' and stepped back for me to come in.

'Modom's in the daining-room,' she said, and trotted back to the kitchen.

'Modom' was grinning all over her face.

'Isn't she a treasure, Sweetie?' she asked, putting her arms round me.

'She looks too good to be true. Did you get any references?'

'I told you she's been at her sister's home, looking after her. She hasn't worked for quite a while and she hasn't the address of the people who last employed her because they've moved.'

'There's one born every day,' I said,

stroking Sylvia's hair.

'Don't be silly, Sweetie. You can see Emily is honest and respectable just by looking at her, and she certainly knows her job.'

'She looks like an escapee from RADA to me,' I said, 'and the name just puts the tin lid on it. Let's eat.'

Five

Emily was a paragon of all the virtues and she lasted exactly two weeks.

To Sylvia she had been the answer to a prayer. She could deal with the phone, adequately if pompously, hand out the prescriptions at the door and do everything required of her in the house efficiently, thereby giving Sylvia a lot more freedom.

Sylvia was delighted at the prospect of introducing Faraday to Tessa Brindley. Not only because, like all newly-weds, she was anxious to see everyone she knew happily married but also because of Emily. We would have our first dinner party as soon as I came back from Edinburgh, at which Emily would wait at table. Being used to more formal service she had, as Sylvia felt, been hiding her light under a bushel. At a dinner party she would really shine.

As far as I was concerned Emily gave me the creeps, and I am sure that I was a constant thorn in her flesh. Like a lilac-trimmed zombie she padded after me in her soft-soled shoes, looking at me reproachfully every time I left my gloves on the hall table or my overcoat slung across the banisters. A tight-lipped martyr, she was forever handing me my auroscope from where I had left it on the drawing-room mantelpiece or informing me unnecessarily that 'Modom' had gone to do her 'little errands' and would be back 'quaite soon.' It wasn't long before I yearned for the unobtrusiveness of Bridget – burnt toast, curlers and all.

When Emily cracked it was in a way that neither of us had expected.

It would not have surprised me if she had disappeared one day with the spoons or made advances to the whisky bottle; she had looked respectable enough in a phoney kind of way for either. But she did nothing of the sort. She merely appeared one morning while we were having breakfast, her eyes ablaze in her usually impassive face, and in a steely voice said: 'Ai'd like to have a word with Modom.'

Since 'Modom' was sitting there, not three feet away, eating her toast, I couldn't see what she was waiting for. I told her to proceed.

Fixing Sylvia with a look of hatred she

said: 'Ai reely thought comin' to a doctor's house that Ai'd be enterin' a gentleman's service. If Ai'd thought for one moment that Modom would stoop to such a thing Ai'd never have considered acceptin' the post.' She was quivering with indignation.

'What is it, Emily?' I asked, getting up and standing near to Sylvia, whom I was afraid Emily was going to strike. 'What's this all about?'

She gave me one of her reproachful looks as if I should have known. 'About the itchin' powder, sir. In mai bed, in mai clothes, in everything Ay possess. Ask Modom; there's not an article she's missed.'

'Emily,' Sylvia said, 'what on earth are you talking about? I haven't been near your room.'

'Ai'm sorry, Modom, but you can smell it a mail away. Smell!' she commanded, and thrust her apron under my nose. I could smell nothing.

'Come upstairs, Emily,' I said, 'and you can show me what it's all about.'

In her room everything seemed to be in order, except that she had packed all her possessions into her two suitcases, which were on the bed.

'Were you thinking of leaving us, Emily?' I said.

'Oh! no, sir. But I dursn't leave anything out, not even mai nightdress. Suppose

Modom were to come in again with the powder. Can't you smell it, sir? It's everywhere.'

I prowled round the room and sniffed at the clothes in her cases. There was nothing at all to be smelled.

'Now, Emily,' I said firmly, 'this is all your imagination. There's no itching powder anywhere and nobody has touched your clothes. I suggest that you unpack your things and get on with your work.'

Emily shook her head. 'Ai couldn't leave mai room,' she said, 'not with all mai things in. Suppose Modom was to come up again!'

It was after nine and I should have started the surgery ten minutes ago. I couldn't waste any more time arguing.

'All right, Emily, you stay here and we'll have a little chat when I've finished the surgery.'

She sat down on the bed with her arms folded and fixed a watchful glance on the door.

Downstairs, I told Sylvia not to disturb her. I would try to sort out the problem after the surgery.

'I'm scared, Sweetie,' she said; 'she seems to have it in for me.'

I blew her a kiss. 'Don't worry, darling. I locked the door on the outside. She looks like a paranoiac to me, probably escaped from a bug-house.'

As it turned out, I wasn't far off the mark.

Emily had spent the last ten years in and out of mental hospitals. She had been released this last time on condition that she remained in the care of her sister. The sister, glad to get rid of her for a bit, had presumed that she could come to no harm by taking a job in a doctor's house, and let her go.

Sorting out this problem in between doing my calls and popping home every now and then to make sure Emily had not escaped, took me the best part of an incredibly busy day. Emily's sister was not on the phone. It was early evening before I contacted her, and then she calmly told me that it wasn't convenient to have Emily back, and since she obviously was having another attack I had better take her straight back to Bolney Thatch, the mental hospital which had become her second home, where they would welcome her with open arms.

It was midnight when, having got rid of Emily, I was tired and irritable and ready for bed.

'For heaven's sake don't take on any more lunatics,' I said to Sylvia. 'I've quite enough to do without wandering round the countryside returning stray maids to mental homes. Kindly see that the next one produces a reference. A personal reference.'

Sylvia yawned. 'It doesn't look as if there'll be a next one for some time. None of the agencies has got a soul, unless we want a footman. And you may be quite sure that I shall examine the pedigree of any future applicants. I've no wish to be murdered in my bed.'

I put out the light.

'Mind you,' Sylvia said, 'it's a pity.'

'What?'

'About Emily. She certainly knew her job.'

'So did Crippen,' I said. 'Goodnight!'

Two days before I was due to leave for Edinburgh and the refresher course, I still had not got a locum to look after the practice while I was away, and we had found no one to replace Emily. It began to look extremely doubtful that I would ever get there. The BMA said they were doing their best, and there was just a possibility that they might have somebody for me by the end of the day. They were trying to contact him.

Rather depressed by the situation, as I was looking forward to going to Edinburgh, I did my calls hoping that the person the BMA had in mind would be more suitable than the last doctor they had sent me.

His name had been Doctor O'Brien and he had arrived one Friday afternoon at the end of Emily's first week with us.

'There's a personage to see you, Doctor,' Emily had announced, intercepting my gloves on their way to the hall table, as I came from my rounds. 'A Doctor O'Brien if mai ears didn't deceive me. Ai put him in the drawin'-room.' She sniffed in a particular way she had, and I wondered what poor Doctor O'Brien had done to incur her displeasure.

It didn't take me long to find out.

I thought it was a little strange when I found Doctor O'Brien, not sitting on one of the chairs as one would expect, but perched on a console table, with his legs dangling. He was singing. He did jump down as soon as he saw me and, weaving his unsteady way towards me across the roses on the carpet, pumped my hand heavily.

''Tis a pleasure to make your acquaintance, Docthor,' he said, his breath nearly anæsthetising me as he spoke, 'and 'tis a dream of a set-up you have here, quiet as the grave, or Killarney on a summer morn.'

I extricated my hand from his leaning grip and he nearly fell over.

'Doctor O'Brien,' I said. He held up his hand.

'I know, boy, I know. You're thinking I'm a trifle inebriated. 'Tis not so. 'Tis not so. To be honest with you,' he lowered his voice confidentially, 'I'm sufferin' from a rare complaint affectin' me balance mechanism. Picked it up in the East when I was surgeon on His Majesty's Ship...'

'Doctor O'Brien,' I said more firmly, coming towards him. He pushed me away.

'There's no need to apologise, boy. When I

was young, like you, still fresh from Queen's, I too had me difficulties with diagnoses. I remember once in County Down – of course, I had me own practice, then...'

'About the locum, Doctor,' I said, intending to tell him the vacancy was already filled.

'Ah! yes, the locum. In me last post 'twas all indostrial, a sad town hoddled 'neath the smoking chimneys, one church, one cinema and twenty-one public houses!'

I took his arm. 'I'm afraid the vacancy is already filled,' I said, propelling him towards the door. 'The BMA must have made a mistake.'

'Yes, yes,' he said amiably, 'and no hard feelings, Doctor, though 'tis a lovely set-up you have here.' He eyed the cocktail cabinet. 'If you'll not mind I'll take a drop of me medicine.' He took a flask from his pocket and enjoyed a long swig of whisky. 'Mist. soda sal. cum colchicum,' he said; 'fine for the creaking joints.'

Watching him weave his unsteady way down the path, his shiny suit hanging loosely from his bony frame, I could not help feeling sorry for him. I wondered what had happened that had made him take to drink and set him on the dreary job of drifting from locum to locum. In his student days he must surely have been as carefree as the rest of his year, a sponge for knowledge and convinced of a brilliant medical future.

He turned the corner, and I wondered if he was aware that his path from now on lay only downhill or if the whisky bottle still beckoned him with a rosy mirage.

Pulling myself together, I realised that feeling sorry for Doctor O'Brien was getting me no nearer to Edinburgh, and went in to phone the BMA and tell them what had happened.

It was now two weeks since I had seen Doctor O'Brien and there had so far been no other applicants for the job.

At the end of the afternoon, as I came home and saw no car outside the house, I presumed that the BMA had failed to contact the person they had told me about, and that the refresher course would have to manage without me.

When Sylvia told me that a Doctor Cataract was waiting to see me it cheered me up considerably.

Doctor Cataract was wearing a duffle coat and had arrived on foot. He was a fine upright figure of an old man with an impressive mane of white hair. He had retired, he told me, from his own practice which he had had for many years, and now took on short locums whenever he felt again the itch to work. He was, he assured me, in spite of his years, in perfect health, and I had to admit that he looked it. Remembering the unfortunate Doctor O'Brien, I looked carefully at the references he produced. They all seemed impeccable and could, he told me, be confirmed by telephone with the principals who had written them.

There was one thing only about Doctor Cataract that worried me a little. He not only had no car but was unable to drive. He walked, he said, everywhere, and the BMA had told him that my practice was all within a fairly close area.

'I shall bring my bicycle,' he said, 'for emergencies.'

'Have you always managed like that, Doctor Cataract?' I asked, curious.

'Always. I like the exercise. I consider the motor car dangerous and unhealthy.'

'Yes, but what about emergencies?'

'As you know,' he said, 'there are very few situations in general practice in which immediate attention is essential, except in the eyes of the patient and his relatives. The fact is that I usually find the little wait to be beneficial; the convulsion subsides, the nosebleed stops, the patient on the floor returns to consciousness. The panic has passed and the situation is more easily dealt with.'

'True,' I agreed, 'but what about an accident or a perforated ulcer?'

'Should something like that occur,' Dr Cataract said calmly, 'I should possibly take a taxi or beg a lift from a passing car.'

'And at night?'

'Come, come, Doctor,' he said. 'I have been in general practice for nearly fifty years and I assure you I haven't yet lost a patient through dilatoriness. There is always a way to get there. You have seen my references.'

'Forgive me,' I said, not really convinced; 'it's just that not to get about by car today seems a little strange.' I changed the subject. 'Have you your own case?' I asked him, 'or shall I leave you mine?'

'I never carry a case,' he said; 'I find them weighty and superfluous.'

He reached into the bulging pockets of his duffle coat and from their depths produced two syringes in sterile containers, several ampoules of morphia and pethidine, a rubber-capped vial of adrenaline, an auroscope, a prescription pad, three or four tiny tins containing tablets of sedatives, a polythene bag in which I could see a bandage, a quantity of cotton-wool and some gauze.

'All I carry in my hand,' he said, 'is my sphygmomanometer. If necessary.'

I could not but admire him. He seemed to have reduced general practice to a fine art. Despite what had appeared at first to be major drawbacks, I felt that my patients would be safe in the seemingly unperturbable if unorthodox hands of Doctor Cataract. He was also a pleasant character to leave around the house with Sylvia for two weeks.

Sylvia, having given him a cup of tea while

he was waiting for me, thought he was an 'absolute darling' and was very sensible to do all his visits on foot. She was always telling me I didn't get enough exercise as I spent most of my time in the car, but woman-like ignored completely the fact that at least once and often twice a week I walked some five or six miles round the golf course.

We had for the moment shelved the problem of our new car. In spite of George Leech's repeated warnings that there was very little life left in my present rattle-trap, we had come to the conclusion that we could not really afford a new one.

When I had first, as H H Brindley advised me, discussed the matter with Sylvia, she said:

'I once went out with a man who had the most divine car. I think it was an Aston Martin, and it had real leopard upholstery.'

I explained as simply as I could that I was a humble National Health practitioner, and that even if every one of my patients paid me pre-Health Scheme private fees I still wouldn't be able to afford an Aston Martin. We then had a long discussion about the 'cake' provided by the private patient, compared with the bread and butter of the panel, and I made up my mind, now that I was established, to build up this side of my practice. There were many people in the district, I knew, who preferred to pay private fees rather than wait in crowded surgeries, and I didn't see why I shouldn't have my share.

Convinced of the impossibility of an Aston Martin with leopard upholstery or a Mercedes Benz, which was her second choice, Sylvia had gone from the sublime to the ridiculous and said what about one of those little bubble cars. She got quite enthusiastic about how much petrol I would be able to save, but when I pointed out that she also liked to be taken out occasionally her enthusiasm disappeared.

Since the thing that had spurred me to action on the car question was the comings and goings of the obnoxious Archibald Compton in his superior Allard, and not the increasing unnroadworthiness of my own car, I decided that in the interests of a good few hundred pounds I would have to swallow my inferiority complex and until my finances improved look the other way.

Now, Sylvia decided, the answer to the problem was simple. If my car finally gave up the ghost, I could be like Doctor Cataract and walk!

Six

Edinburgh was beautiful, the refresher course interesting and the golf superb.

After the difficulties of fixing up the various arrangements at home I could hardly believe that I had actually managed to get there at all.

The problem of the practice had been solved with the appearance of Doctor Cataract, but up to the day before I was due to leave we were still maidless, and I couldn't leave Sylvia alone and tied to the house for a fortnight.

In the maid line, we were willing to settle for anything from a husky Swede to an Italian peasant. Our advertisements had brought answers only from colonels' daughters who were willing to do a little 'light' housework in exchange for a room, or women who were willing to do anything at all provided we could accommodate their various small infants. The agencies assured us that help would be forthcoming, but that we mustn't be impatient. 'We can get you someone from the Continent within two months, or someone might walk into the office today.' Needless to say they never did walk into the office 'today' or any other day; or if they did they were never rerouted in our direction. We had to remain satisfied with the varied assurances that our requirements would be 'put at the top of the list,' 'borne in mind,' 'taken good care of,' and 'given priority.' Meanwhile we had placed a firm order for a Dutch girl with an unpronounceable name whose passport photograph revealed nothing except that in company with many of her countrywomen she had a stolid, moonlike face. She was not due to arrive, however, for many weeks. At the last moment Sylvia thought of Molly.

Molly was the actress friend with whom she had shared a flat before our marriage.

'She'll come like a shot if she's "resting,"' Sylvia said. And fortunately Molly, who was inclined to be 'resting' more often than she was working, was, by a strange coincidence, waiting for a part she had been promised in a West End production to materialise. Knowing Molly, we were sure that the part would most likely not be given to her within the next two weeks, if it existed at all. She said she would be delighted to come and keep Sylvia company while I was away.

At ten o'clock on the evening before I was to leave they were both still packing for me, although I had explained several times that I was only going to Edinburgh for a fortnight and not on a world tour. My protestations fell on deaf ears. Sylvia was adding the umpteenth pair of pants to a formidable collection of shirts, collars, vests, handkerchiefs, ordinary socks and golf socks, and Molly was trying to find some reasonable numbers among what she said was a collection of 'perfectly deadly' ties. I had told them several times and in various tones of voice, that before I was married it took me about two minutes to pack, and they had been at it for at least two hours. It made no difference, though, and I gave up trying to compete with the girlish chatter and bursts of hysterical laughter when they tried to shut the too-full case and was glad when I had to go out on a call.

At midnight I was polishing my golf clubs in the kitchen. Sylvia and Molly, exhausted by the effort of getting me packed, had gone to bed.

I was just burnishing my favourite wood to conker-brightness and hoping that Archibald Compton would not pinch any of my patients while I was away, when I felt two arms entwine themselves round my neck.

'Sweetie,' Sylvia said, 'you know you've got to be up at six!'

'I know, but I couldn't go with dirty equipment.'

'I don't believe you're going to any lectures at all. You're just going to play golf.'

'It depends on the weather,' I said.

Sylvia kissed me. 'I shall miss you,' she said.

'I've been thinking all day. It's a funny feeling, isn't it? Perhaps I'd better not go.'

'After all the packing I've done so beautifully?'

'Seriously, darling. I like being married. I don't want to leave you.'

'Think of the golf courses.'

'I still don't.'

'Then put down that stupid golf club and prove it.'

I put down the golf club and almost missed my train.

I had reserved a room at the large hotel near the station, and on the first evening made the mistake of sitting in the vast morgue-like lounge to have my coffee. The hotel visitors seemed to be either doctors for the postgraduate course or commercial travellers, and I hadn't yet discovered which were which.

The bald-headed, tubby little man wearing a navy-blue suit and shy brown shoes, who was sharing the little coffee table with me, waited only until I had taken the first sip of lukewarm, treacle-like coffee.

'Will I buy ye a drink, Doctor?' he boomed at me suddenly.

'How do you know I'm a doctor?' I said, putting down my cup in surprise.

'Well, ye're no one of the boys, so it wasna'

difficult.' He snapped his fingers at a passing, seedy-looking waiter. 'Two brandies, Jock.' He winked at me. 'And mebbe we can afterwards go into the bar. I'll introduce ye to one or two of the boys. What did ye say ye're name was again?'

'I didn't say,' I said, 'and although it's extremely kind of you I don't really want a brandy just now.'

He held up a pudgy hand. 'It's a real pleasure,' he said, 'to buy a drink for you, Doctor. I've a great admiration for your profession and I've had the misfortune to see a great many medical men in my time.' He shuffled his chair in a little closer and leaned towards me conspiratorially. 'It's ma liver,' he said, 'though to tell ye the truth it's no playing me up as it was in fifty-five. No, mebbe it was fifty-four... Yes, fifty-four it was; I remember I was in Glasgie and the specialist there...'

I looked round for some means of escape, but I didn't know a soul and everyone was sitting round motionless as stuffed dummies and silent under the soporific spell of brown plush and potted plants.

The brandy came and went. I returned the compliment. After three-quarters of an hour my friend had exhausted his liver, hypertension and query gall-bladder and we had progressed to yarns.

His face was flushed and his little eyes

warming to the theme.

'Have ye heard the one about the honeymoon couple and the wee dog? Well, this honeymoon couple...'

A young man with glasses at the end of his nose was loping by our table. I was desperate. 'Hey, Blanchard!' I called, catching at the edge of his sports jacket. He looked round in amazement, but by the time he had taken the pipe out of his mouth to protest, I had excused myself to my companion, halted in mid-joke, and thanked him for his company. 'Must have a word with old Blanchard,' I said, 'we did our midder together at St Albans.' I put a matey arm round 'Blanchard's' shoulders and hauled him out of the lounge.

'Blanchard,' once he had recovered from the shock of being accosted so rudely, was understanding. His name was Musgrove, he had a third share in a practice in Dulwich and, most important of all, he had brought his golf clubs. I didn't go near the mausoleum of a lounge for the rest of my stay and spent much of my time with Musgrove, with whom it turned out I had much in common. He had also not long been married and we had plenty to discuss.

I had been in Edinburgh only three days before I became acquainted with Iris.

My bedroom was on the top floor of the hotel at the end of a long, long corridor.

Like the rest of the hotel, it was large, chilly and gloomy. The bed was brass, the carpet threadbare and the curtains green velvet. My tea was brought each morning by a grey-haired chambermaid with whiskers on her chin. I saw her for approximately two minutes each day, when she plonked down the tea-tray after much rattling at the door with keys, mumbled 'Good-morning' and swept back the curtains, releasing little clouds of dust into the room. On the fourth morning I didn't even open my eyes to greet this vision and was surprised when I heard the tray put gently on my bedside table and then a gay voice calling:

'Good-morning, Doctor! And a beautiful morning, too. It's a little bit late, so you'd better wake up or you'll be late for your lecture.'

I opened my eyes and was almost blinded by a bush of bright red hair close to my face. Tender hands were replacing the eiderdown from where it had slipped on to the floor.

'I'm Iris,' she said, and giggled. 'I should have done you all along but I've been off with a septic finger so old Ma Mackenzie's being doing you. I don't know why they stuck you up here. We usually put the doctors on the first and second.'

She sat down on the bed and poured out my tea. While I drank it she wandered round the room picking up the dirty socks and handkerchiefs I had left strewn about and collecting the assortment of golf tees from the dressing-table and mantelpiece.

'I'll find you a box for those,' she said, 'and I'll take your dirty washing.' She picked up Sylvia's photograph from the dressing-table. 'Married?'

'Yes.'

'Pretty, isn't she? I nearly got married once.'

'What happened?'

'I came to my senses. I don't like being tied down. I like to move around.'

'How old are you?'

'Eighteen.' She sighed. 'I love men. And babies.'

I thought it was about time that I got the eighteen-year-old Iris, with her red hair and her impudent figure, out of my room.

'I'd better get up,' I said.

'I'll run your bath. You've got Metabolic Bone Disease at nine o'clock. Professor Popper. It'll be fine for golf this evening, though. It always is when we get a misty morning. Nice and hot?'

'What's that?'

'The bath. Don't worry, I'll Vim it first.'

'Yes, nice and hot.'

After she had gone, with a shake of her jolly posterior which crackled her white apron, the room seemed quiet. Somehow, though, it didn't seem so drab.

My own mother couldn't have looked after me better. Iris did my washing, brushed my suits, sewed a button on my shirt, found a brighter bulb for the sad, fringed light, kept me informed as to my timetable and told me the best places to eat. My hotel bedroom began to feel like home.

Sylvia's letters were wonderful and arrived every day. It was almost worth being separated from her to see how much she loved me, written down on paper. She wrote in detail about the practice and the progress of Doctor Cataract, who appeared to be dealing quite competently with everything. She wrote like a seasoned doctor's wife: 'We had two coronaries in one day and Billy Jones did turn out to be glandular fever. Mrs Christopher had her baby two weeks early, a girl! Isn't it a shame? She did so want a little boy. Doctor Cataract is frightfully conscientious and goes trotting off as soon as a call comes in. He is very neat and tidy and always throws his empty ampoules straight into the bin. Please note!

'Molly has been doing the cooking and it is like old times in the flat – more 'tin-opener' than anything. We are having an exotic diet of snails, lichees, fonds d'artichauts and, of course, Molly's renowned spaghetti with a sauce containing just about every herb under the sun. To be quite honest, Sweetie, I had got out of the habit of this haphazard eating and will be quite pleased to make you a straightforward steak and chips when you come home.

'Molly thinks it's wonderful to be a doctor's wife because there's never a dull moment. You would laugh if you heard her answer the phone. The patients must think we change our staff every day, because she never uses the same accent twice. They get everything from Eliza Dolittle (Act One) to Lady Bracknell. Sometimes she gets quite carried away and booms, "Oh! My dear, how perfectly frightful," in that deep bass voice of hers when some poor woman rings to say the baby has a napkin rash!

'I am waiting for a letter from Moonface to say exactly when she is arriving...'

On a Saturday at the end of our first week, we had a free day with no lectures. Musgrove and I decided that we would go on a shopping expedition to find presents to take home to our wives. It was a job which neither of us relished, as we were unused to shopping and had no idea of what we wanted. We set out gloomily after breakfast and plodded doggedly up and down Princess Street looking in the windows. We rejected handbags as too expensive; it wasn't, after all, a birthday or an anniversary; tray cloths as too plebeian, perfume as too bewildering, stockings as pointless as neither of us knew the size, gloves (ditto), tartan tins of shortbread as not good enough and books as obtainable more cheaply from the library. At eleven-thirty Musgrove yawned and said what about some coffee, and we sat miserably in a café making futile suggestions to each other and wishing we had a little more experience in dealing with wives.

Our conversation went something like this:

'Tartan scarves.'

'Tartan kilts.'

'Tartan socks.'

'Stuff to put on their faces.'

'Slippers. Tartan.'

'Cookery books,' Musgrove said meaningly.

We drank our coffee. I tried to think. Sylvia was always saying 'I must get this,' or 'that,' or 'the other,' but since I was rarely paying complete attention I was unable to think of one item she had declared indispensable to her well-being.

Musgrove had gone into a trance. Suddenly he put down his coffee cup with a bang. His glasses, always at the end of his nose, fell into a plate of shortbread.

'Nightdresses!' he shouted, his face illuminated.

The manageress, a green band crosswise over her heaving bosom, hastened up.

'Was there something, sir?' she said, quivering with indignation at the obscene word Musgrove had let loose in her restaurant.

We paid the bill and fled.

This time we moved eagerly. We passed acres and acres of tartan kilts, scarves, gloves, stoles, ties, slippers, coats, hats, comb cases and suitcases before we found what we were looking for.

The window was tastefully decorated: brassières, stuffed and unstuffed, chopped-off torsos wearing roll-ons, panties in colours of the rainbow, and in the centre, on a waxen-breasted dummy, a black, diaphanous nightdress.

'That's the one,' Musgrove said, pointing, and a woman, who had been standing behind us as we looked in the window, said 'Disgusting!' and walked quickly on.

The manageress, despite her grey hair and forbidding appearance, was helpful. Since we had no idea of the size worn by either of our 'Madams' she lined up four of her young assistants. Musgrove chose a simpering Miss Jeannie, from which I came to the conclusion that Mrs Musgrove was short and dumpy, and I picked on Miss Marjorie as being as near as I could tell, without actually putting my arms around her, approximately the same size as Sylvia. That problem being resolved we selected a style; black nylon trimmed with pink roses for Sylvia and black nylon trimmed with blue ribbon for Mrs Musgrove. Well pleased with our purchases, we each clutched our tartan carrier bags bearing the legend 'Frillywear (Lingerie), Ltd,' and made for the door. The manageress saw us out.

'Good-day to you, Doctor,' she said to Musgrove. I looked at her in astonishment. 'And to you, Doctor.'

'How do you think she knew?' Musgrove said, outside.

'Haven't a clue. Unless it was because we didn't blush. Let's get rid of these damned things and go up to Braid Hills. We've time for a full round today.'

Back at the hotel I slung the 'Frillywear (Lingerie), Ltd,' bag on top of the wardrobe and started looking for my golf socks when Iris came in with a telegram. It was from Sylvia and said:

'Moonface unable to come, mother ill. Any maids Edinburgh? Love S.'

'Is it serious?' Iris asked in the manner of all the working classes associating telegrams with illness and death.

An idea leaped into my head.

'Iris,' I said, 'how would you like to come and work for us? We've been let down, and it's awfully difficult in a doctor's house. It means my wife can never get out.'

Iris considered.

'Is she expecting?'

'Who, Sylvia? No.'

'Pity. I like babies.'

'I'm terribly sorry,' I said.

'Well, never mind. I'll come till you get someone.' She looked at Sylvia's photograph. 'She looks nice.

By the door she shook a warning finger at me. 'I don't promise to stay, though. I've got itchy feet. I'll go and give my notice to the housekeeper.' She gave me a cheeky look. 'I never stay here after the doctors have gone, anyway. The commercials are too troublesome.' She winked suggestively. 'If you're looking for your clean golf socks they're in your bag. Try not to make such a potato in them next time.'

I was sure Sylvia would be more pleased with Iris than with her nightie.

Seven

The course finished on Friday night. Musgrove and I, anxious to have a last round of golf, decided to leave after lunch on Saturday.

On Saturday morning the rain literally fell out of a dour Scottish sky. Reluctant as we were, both Musgrove and I came to the conclusion that our waterproof hats, jackets, trousers and gaily striped umbrellas were no match for this type of downpour. Sadly we abandoned the hope of the new balls we might have won and decided to take an early train home. I thought I would surprise Sylvia and didn't ring her about the change of plan. I paid my hotel bill and told Iris to get ready.

In London I said goodbye to Musgrove. We agreed that we had had a splendid fortnight: had profited by the lectures, which had been most interesting, and played some excellent golf. We exchanged telephone numbers and firm assurances that we would keep in touch with each other. Musgrove went off carrying his clubs and his 'Frillywear (Lingerie), Ltd,' underwear bag, his glasses as usual at the end of his nose. Iris was carrying my carrier bag, as I had forgotten to pack it and she had rescued it at the last minute from the top of the wardrobe. We gathered our belongings and got into a taxi.

It was half-past five when we pulled up outside my house, behind a white Jaguar. My first thought was that Doctor Cataract had been collecting wealthy patients. My second thought was Wilfred Pankrest. I remembered the car well from the time when Sylvia had been engaged to Wilfred and had brought him to tea with me. On getting out of the taxi, my suspicions were confirmed. With the typical Pankrest love of ostentation his car bore the number plates WP 1. With an upsurge of schoolboy desires I longed to let the air out of his tyres; with a swift return to manhood and reality I wondered what the blazes he was doing in my house, presumably with Sylvia, while I was away. My mood of gaiety, nurtured all the way from Edinburgh by the thought of coming home and seeing Sylvia again, disappeared. I was angry. I never had been able to stand the sight of Wilfred's upper-class, chinless, champagne-filled face, and Sylvia knew it. 'Come on, Iris,' I snarled, and I picked up the two heaviest cases.

As we stepped into the porch the door opened and Wilfred stepped out, cramming his soft green trilby on his aristocratic head. Sylvia followed him out to see him off. There was a moment of complete silence and immobility as Iris and I stared at Sylvia and Wilfred, and then the tableau broke up.

'Sweetie!' Sylvia said.

Wilfred said, 'Good Lord!'

I said grimly, 'We caught an earlier train,' and Iris, staring open-mouthed at Wilfred, said, 'Ooh, I've seen your picture in the *Mirror!*' and in her excitement at meeting Britain's Number One Playboy face to face, clutched at the wrong end of the 'Frillywear (Lingerie), Ltd,' carrier bag. The black nylon nightdress, looking even more diaphanous than it had in the shop, slid sighingly out and wafted down to drape itself over Wilfred's elegant, pointed-toed, brown suede shoes. We were all again transfixed – Iris with horror, Sylvia with suspicion, Wilfred with amusement and myself with rage at Wilfred for messing up my homecoming. Somebody had to act. I picked up the nightdress, shook Wilfred's codfishy hand and said it was nice to have seen him, hustled Iris and the cases over the threshold and shut the front door firmly. Molly came running out of the waiting-room.

'Thank heavens you're back!' she proclaimed dramatically.

'Why? What's the matter?'

Molly fluttered her not inconsiderable eyelashes. 'There's some poor soul having a baby and doing some quite unmentionable things. The midwife has sent the husband down twice.'

'Where's Doctor Cataract?'

'He's taken Shanks' pony to an insulin coma over at Granville Road.'

'Next time the husband comes tell him to tell the midwife I'm not home yet and she'll get someone else or send her into hospital.'

'But I've got the poor man in the waiting-room,' Molly said, 'and he knows you're home. He saw you from the window.' She lowered her eyelids and said in a gallery-reaching dirge: 'There are complications.'

Tired and angry, I went towards the waiting-room. Sylvia ran after me. 'Don't bother me now,' I snapped.

'I wasn't going to,' she said, and undraped the nightdress from where it dangled over my arm.

Mrs Taylor took her time over producing a squalling nine-pound infant. By the time Sister Snead and I had sewn her up, cleaned her up, and left her sitting up, drinking a cup of tea, it was after nine. I felt weary, dirty and irritable, and only partly mollified by the fact that Mrs Taylor had named the baby after me.

At home, Doctor Cataract was waiting for me, ready to hand the practice back. He sat with me in the dining-room while I had my dinner, and as I shovelled in mouthfuls of Molly's risotto in which were hidden numerous unidentifiable objects, he told me what had been happening while I had been away. Everything appeared to have gone smoothly. The old man had coped with everything, made meticulous notes about each patient he had seen, and taken everything in his stride. When I had finished some cold, quivery, lemon-flavoured concoction that was my dessert, I settled up with Doctor Cataract and he put on his duffle coat, anxious to be going home to bed.

In the hall he dropped his voice conspiratorially and put his hand into his pocket.

'There was just one thing, Doctor,' he said, and handed me an opened pale blue envelope. 'You did tell me to open all the correspondence, but I think this one was rather personal.' He looked at me from under his bushy grey eyebrows. 'I didn't like to give it to your wife.'

I drew the single sheet of blue paper from the envelope. The writing was illiterate, backward-sloping. 'My darling Brown Eyes,' I read, 'I'm worried not seeing you...'

I smiled at Doctor Cataract. 'That's all right,' I said. 'It's only some psychopathic girl who imagines she's in love with me.'

The eyebrows shot up, sweeping away the frown as they went.

'I'm so glad, my boy. So glad. You've such a charming wife. Indeed charming.' He held out his hand and, stuffing Renee Trotter's letter into my pocket, I thanked him for all he had done.

'It's been a pleasure, Doctor,' the old man said, 'and I trust that you'll find everything in good order.'

From the morning-room I heard strange noises. I listened outside the door. A cultured voice was saying: '...spread on toast it's wonderful! Add it to your soups, stews, gravies. Give it to your children when they want a snack. You can be sure then that they've had more than a treat, for Boxo Beef Spread is a jarful of vitamins...' It sounded like the television, but since we hadn't one I opened the door curiously. Molly was standing on the coffee table holding one of my Elastoplast tins before her and grinning brightly from ear to ear. When she saw me the smile faded.

'Oh! it's you,' she said, and jumped down on to the floor. 'I was just rehearsing. I'm on the Boxo stand at the Family Fare Exhibition next week.' She held out the Elastoplast tin and put back her charming leer. 'Won't you try some Boxo Beef Spread?' she breathed, advancing seductively towards me. 'Jarful of vitamins!'

'Blast Boxo!' I said. 'Where's Sylvia?'

'Gone to bed.'

'I'm going, too. Goodnight, Molly.'

She held up her tin. 'A little Boxo in a glass of hot milk will ensure sound sleep,' she said hopefully. I shut the door.

In the bedroom Sylvia was sitting up in bed in the nightdress she had worn, for a short while, on our wedding night. She looked very lovely and I almost forgot how angry and tired I was.

'Sweetie,' she said, and held out her arms. 'I haven't even had a chance to kiss you.'

I stayed away from the bed and began deliberately to take the small change out of my pockets and put it neatly on the mantelpiece. I came straight to the point.

'What was Wilfred doing here?' I snapped.

Sylvia, snubbed, her arms still in the air, pouted.

'He came to tea.'

'Well, what were you doing having that miserable, gormless, nightclub-hopper here to tea the minute my back was turned? It was just as well I took an earlier train or I might never have found out what was going on.'

'Don't be ridiculous,' Sylvia said. 'You know perfectly well there was nothing going on.' She lowered her voice: 'Don't be cross, Sweetie. Come here and say hallo.'

If it hadn't been for the long and tiring train journey, followed by my struggle on behalf of Master Taylor, followed by my long talk with Doctor Cataract, I might have left it at that. I was thoroughly worked up, though, and my eyes were sore with weariness.

'I won't have that drip in my house!' I shouted. 'And if I can't go away for two weeks knowing I can trust my own wife...'

'Don't be so disgusting,' Sylvia said, swinging her legs out of bed and advancing towards me. 'There's absolutely no need to be insulting. I happen to be your wife, not a member of your harem, and if I can't invite a friend to tea without first asking your permission...'

'It's a pity you didn't marry Wilfred,' I said scathingly, a little demon inside driving me on, 'since you appear to be so fond of him.'

Sylvia followed me into the bathroom, where I put in the plug and turned both taps on.

'That's just what I should have done,' Sylvia yelled at me above the noise of the water, then trailed back after me into the bedroom. 'At least I shouldn't have been a slave to the telephone morning, noon and night and hear nothing but moans, groans and complaints all day. Everybody I talk to is ill, and you complain when I invite a few healthy people to tea.'

I snorted derisively as I thought of Wilfred's anæmic exterior.

'If you call that weedy specimen healthy...' I collected my pyjamas. Sylvia followed me again into the bathroom.

'There's nothing the matter with Wilfred,' she said, standing over me as I scrubbed my back with the loofah, 'and if there's anyone who has reason for complaint, it's me.'

I showered off the soap with the hand-spray and looked at her, questioningly.

She folded her arms. 'If you expect me to believe that story about bringing Iris back because you thought she'd be a good maid,' she said, 'you must think I'm a little bit dim. She's no more a maid than I am; and if she is a maid, what's she doing with that ... that ... nothing of a nightdress?' She advanced and stood on the bathmat. 'Don't tell me she brought that to impress the wallpaper in the maid's bedroom.'

I opened my mouth to explain about the nightdress, but she didn't give me a chance. 'I thought your letters from Edinburgh were a bit short. Now I know why. I don't suppose you had much time to spare...'

'Sylvia,' I said with icy dignity, 'do you mind getting off the bathmat so that I can get out of the bath?'

She moved towards the door.

'Get out of the blasted bath,' she shouted, her self-control going, 'and you ought to be jolly well ashamed of yourself, carrying on with some hotel chambermaid after we've only been married three months.' The tears were rolling down her face and her voice rose in a crescendo. 'You'll be sorry for treating me like this just now,' she sobbed, 'jolly sorry.'

'Don't try to make out that I'm in the wrong,' I said, rubbing my back vigorously. 'Remember, it's Wilfred that started all this. And why should I be sorry for treating you like this just now?'

Sylvia took the corner of the bath-towel to wipe her eyes.

'Because I'm going to have a baaaabee,' she howled, and ran from the bathroom, slamming the door behind her.

I wasn't sure if I had heard properly. Suddenly my temper evaporated. My hands started to shake: I shook talcum powder over the floor instead of myself, struggled into my pyjamas, putting both feet into the same pyjama leg, and lost one end of the cord in its socket. Anxious to lose no more time, I gathered the baggy pants round me and, without stopping to put on my slippers, ran on weak legs into the bedroom.

'What was that you said?' I demanded, addressing my remark to a heaving mound of bedclothes.

The bedclothes only heaved more. Taking hold of the covers, I flung them back.

Sylvia turned on her tummy and buried her face in the pillow.

'A baby,' she said. 'A B–A–B–Y, baby.'

I hesitated. 'Don't be ridiculous,' I said, uncertainly. 'How could you be pregnant without me knowing? It only happens like that in books or women's magazines where certain physiological functions are unmentionable.'

A muffled voice from the depths of the pillow said: 'You seem to forget you've been away for two weeks.'

'But why didn't you tell me if you were suspicious?'

There was a fresh wail. 'I wanted to give you a surpriiiise...'

I thought about it. 'You may not be pregnant at all.'

She spun round and sat bolt upright.

'Mr Know-All,' she said. 'I beg your pardon, Doctor Know-All. I had a test: Doctor Cataract arranged it.' She looked up at me with her red-rimmed eyes, in which fresh tears were welling.

'And for heaven's sake stop standing there trying to look dignified with your trousers liable to fall down at any moment.' She started to giggle and then to laugh hysterically. I sat down on the bed and put my arms round her.

'Sylvia,' I said gently, 'shsh.'

She buried her head in my shoulder and I waited, stroking her hair, until she had stopped shaking; then I held her away from me and looked at her.

'Sylvia,' I said, 'is it true?'

She nodded. 'Are you pleased?'

I nodded my head and kissed her, so overcome with the thought of becoming a father that I was quite unable to talk.

After a while I said, 'I could kill myself.'

'Why, Sweetie?'

'For shouting at you like that.'

'I understand. You were tired.'

'You should have told me about the baby.'

'I didn't have a chance.'

'Of course you didn't.'

'I was so excited about your coming home so that I could tell you.'

'I could hardly wait to get here.'

'We're so stupid, aren't we?'

'Inane.' I turned out the light and got into bed.

We talked, until we had no more to say, about the prospects of parenthood. We were just drifting off to sleep when I remembered something.

'Sylvia,' I said. 'Mm?'

'What *was* Wilfred doing here?'

She laughed. 'Well, you know before you went to Edinburgh you were talking about getting more private patients?'

'Yes.'

'Well, Wilfred knows so many society people who do nothing but call in the doctor morning, noon and night and pay vast fees without blinking, that I thought he might be able to recommend a few of his friends to you, so I wanted to give you a surprise.'

'Darling,' I said, 'you're full of surprises.' I kissed her. 'It's absolutely sweet of you, dear, but I'd really rather you didn't go round touting for patients. Even private ones.'

'All right,' she said; 'I thought you'd be pleased. Anyway, you'll have to go and see the Hon. Mrs Magnus-Wight, because it's all arranged. Wilfred told me when he came over today.'

'OK,' I said, 'now let's go to sleep.'

'Not so fast, Sweetie. I've explained about Wilfred, but you haven't told me the truth about Iris and the nightie.'

'There's nothing to be told, my love. Iris was truly the chambermaid at the hotel, and I'm sure she'll help you a lot. As for the nightie, I bought it for you. A present from Edinburgh.'

'Sweetie! You actually went into a shop and chose it for me?'

'That's right.'

'Sweetie,' she said. 'I shall wear it every night until it doesn't fit me any more. After that I shall wear it to receive visitors.'

'It's not exactly intended as a hostess gown.'

'Who cares?' said Sylvia. 'Goodnight.'

Eight

As it was the end of the quarter, my post on Monday brought a fat buff envelope containing the medical records of patients who had recently come on my list and, more important, a sheet of ruled white paper which I always looked at anxiously. On this were written the names of patients who had gone off the list. Against each patient's name was a letter, and by referring to the footnote at the bottom of the form the letter could be interpreted as the reason why that particular person was no longer registered with me. The letters were: X – transfer to the list of another doctor in the same area; R – removal to another area; D – death; E – embarkation; and S – enlistment.

Mrs Rumbold, to whom I had refused to give the iron tablets she demanded, was an X; so were her children. Her husband's name was not mentioned, and I gave him a silent vote of thanks for refusing to be as fickle as his wife. The Executive Council did not mention the name of the doctor to whom the patients had transferred, but gave only his official code number. I was familiar with the numbers of all the other practitioners in the district, so it wasn't difficult to deduce that the new, high number against the names of Mrs Rumbold and Co. was my old friend Archibald Compton. According to the list, he had also lured away Mildred Price with her two chronic complaints, who was, poor soul, probably expecting a new doctor to produce a new cure out of his hat; Mrs Schwarz and family, for whom I never did the right thing because 'bei uns ve do alvays dis' when it wasn't 'dot' or the 'udder'; a family who had been on my list but whom I had never seen at all; Mr MacTaggart, who invariably rang for a visit long after I had left on my rounds and was annoyed when I didn't turn up until the afternoon; the Brooks family, with whom for no particular reason I had never seemed to get on; and finally Mr And Mrs Hart and their four children. These last names were the only ones that sent a prickle of irritation through me; I had treated the Hart family for quite a number of complaints, had got on very well with them, and could see no reason at all why they should want to change their doctor. I should be most interested to know why they had all given their cards to Doctor Compton, and would keep a close eye on number 93981.

Refreshed by my two weeks' holiday, I did my morning surgery with new zest. I was polite to everybody, listened without irritation to the longest of long-drawn-out and roundabout histories, and positively exuded bonhomie.

My first patient was a Teddy boy wearing narrow black trousers, a jacket which nearly reached his knees, bright yellow socks and a tie which looked like a piece of black string. His luxuriant growth of hair was dressed in the popular style known, I was told, as the 'elephant's trunk.' The name of this vision was Richard Tenby, commonly known as 'Rocky,' and I had been treating him for a long time for headaches. I had been unable to find a cause for his complaint, and although I suspected the headaches were functional rather than organic in origin, I had recently referred him to the Hospital for Diseases of the Nervous System for further investigation. This was the first time I had seen him since then.

'Well, Rocky,' I said, when he was sitting in front of me, 'how did you get on?'

'OK,' he said.

'Tell me what happened.'

'Well, I see the doc first, see, and 'e arsks me all sorts of things about meself and me work and I tells him I'm a coachbuilder, see. So 'e says well I spec you take it too much to heart see, too fussy like. So I says nah! So 'e says well tell me ackcherly wot you do. So I says I puts in the four screws wot goes under the panels. So 'e says well I spec you very fussy that you got 'em in exackly right, worrying like! So I says nah! I couldn't care less 'cos after the panel's on yer can't even see 'em. So 'e says Oh! Then 'e sticks some pins in me and says can yer feel 'em and I says blimey yes. Then arter that I goes down to where some bird puts wires all over me 'ead and tests me brain, then arter she's finished mucking me abaht I gotta go to the gym see. Well in the gym there's another bird and she throws me a football to relax she says. So I throws it back to 'er and she throws it back to me again. I throws it back to 'er again then arter a bit she says you do this better than wot I do and I says well I do it every Satdey arternoon so she says you don't need to relax so we packs it up.'

'Then what happened?' I said.

'Then I come 'ome.'

'Oh!' I said, 'then I'll be getting a report from the doctor you saw shortly. What can I do for you now.'

'Well,' he said, 'I come abaht me 'ead-aches!'

After Rocky Tenby, Mrs Goodwin came in with her baby, who seemed to be suffering, she said, from stomach-ache. She had given him a 'powder,' but it had seemed to have no effect.

From time immemorial it has been one of a mother's prerogatives to prescribe medicaments for her offspring without taking medical advice. With the advent of the National Health Service and 'free' attention from the doctor, this practice is only a little less common than before. I was always interested to discover how very many of my infant patients received unprescribed medicines for internal use during their first year of life. These medicines consisted in the main of gripe water, teething powders and mixtures, cough mixtures (often the good old-fashioned, home-made mixture of black treacle and vinegar), aspirin and aperients, the old belief in the efficacy of which dies hard. The infants at the receiving end of these administrations seemed to survive the various brews poured with mother's good faith at various times down their unprotesting throats. They were at any rate a great deal luckier than many children in rural districts of France who, up till not so very long ago, were made to eat omelettes containing finely minced-up grilled mouse if they were unfortunate enough to be bed-wetters, a broth of earthworms for worm infestations, or a syrup made of snails or slugs for whooping cough.

Grandma was still, of course, a great believer in red flannel, overheating and copious 'rubbings-in' of the chest. It was often only when all else this good lady did had failed that I was telephoned to enquire whether I was 'sitting,' 'serving,' or 'practising' that day.

I dealt with Baby Goodwin's stomach-ache on slightly more orthodox lines, then started to hurry things up a bit since, according to Mrs Goodwin, the waiting-room was packed.

When I had finished it was after eleven. I did the two most urgent visits on my list, then thought that I had better go and see the Hon. Mrs Magnus-Wight, since Wilfred had promised her I would be there before twelve. At five to twelve I rang the bell of her luxurious flat in West Street. A parlourmaid, the genuine article, not a refugee from Bolney Thatch like our Emily, opened the door and led me into the hall where, she said, I was to wait. 'Meddem,' she said, scarcely allowing her lips to part and looking at me with the greatest disapproval, was 'in the bath.'

I looked ostentatiously at my watch and decided I would give her a few minutes. I was aware that I was now dealing with a different type of patient, who was willing to pay a large fee for the privilege of seeing the doctor at her own convenience. I could not, as I did with my Health Scheme practice, run up the stairs two at a time, listening to the history from mother or relative as I went, examine the patient, prescribe and rush down and out again into the car. The Hon. Mrs Magnus-Wight was paying for the same treatment but with different trimmings. In her case one would have to 'hurry slowly,' giving her the impression that she was my one and only patient and concern. She was paying for me to turn up when she was ready to receive me and would cut me off without a shilling if I turned up, as I often did to my other patients, when I was very busy, before the morning surgery, catching them with the curlers still in their hair and a night-rumpled bed. Usually, once they had recovered from the initial shock of my intrusion and given up trying to unwind their hair when my back was turned, they were only too pleased to get such prompt attention. Not so with the Mrs Magnus-Wights. The GP must wait in the ink-blue-carpeted hall, most probably, I suspected, for no reason at all. The slightest deviation from the norm would, I was sure, require more specialised attention, more letters after the name.

The parlourmaid rustled back and forth to the bedroom. Once with a vase of flowers, once with a cup of coffee, once just to see what I was up to. Since I was picking up a Sèvres ashtray from the table at the time to examine it more closely, she probably felt her vigilance justified.

At a quarter past twelve I was joined by a frayed-cuffed companion, who was placed in a chair facing me. He informed me that he had come to 'chune the pianner' and enquired whether they had given me a cup of tea.

At twelve-thirty I decided that I had waited long enough and prowled down the corridor, my feet sinking into the carpet, in search of the ray of sunshine who had let me in. She gave me a scathing look for my impatience but said that 'Meddem' would see me now.

The Hon. Mrs Magnus-Wight was draped in blue velvet on a chaise longue draped in pink velvet. She was on the telephone. I put my case down on the bed, from where it was promptly snatched by the parlourmaid and plonked on the floor, and prowled round the room making impatient noises. A lily-white hand waved me imperiously to a tiny, squiggly, pink velvet chair by the door. I ignored the invitation and continued prowling. I waited while she agreed to provide a case of whisky for the tombola at the charity dance – '...when I think of those poor blind babies it makes my blood run cold...' – that Philippe was certainly the only hairdresser to go to now, absolutely no one who was anyone went to Maurice any more, and that certainly they would all go together to that new American musical – 'afterwards supper at the Rose Room, yes?'

My prowlings grew noisier and noisier and after she had said 'Darling, I really must go now,' for about the fifteenth time, she put the phone down.

Turning to me, she looked down her nose and held out her hand.

'Well,' she snapped, 'have you brought the patterns?'

She was looking at my case. For a moment I wondered whether she had expected me to provide her with samples of various illnesses from which she could choose one that sounded attractive.

'What patterns?' I said.

'For the curtains. I've no time to waste this morning. You are from Staples, aren't you?'

I explained that I was not from Staples and told her who I was, and she looked only slightly less annoyed. She was still mystified until I mentioned Wilfred. She thought for a long moment and then said: 'Oh! Willie Pankrest! Now I remember. Of course it was Willie who told me about you. You cured that ghastly bore Lord ffanshaw of his boils, I believe; some new stuff, something "ozone" wasn't it?'

She was clearly confusing me with someone else. I waited until she had finished rambling and then I asked her what was the matter.

'Nothing,' she said, as far as she knew. She felt all her limbs as if to see if she had overlooked a broken one.

'But why did you send for me?' I asked. 'Mr Pankrest said you wanted me to call.'

Her blue eyes, ringed with a fence of black mascara, popped wide.

'But that was *last* week,' she shrilled. 'I can't remember exactly what it was I was suffering from at that dinner of Poppy's; I was sitting next to Willie, delightful boy, but anyway, whatever it was, it's quite, quite better.'

I picked up my case.

She sat forward. 'Oh! no. Don't go,' she said. 'While you're here you might as well give me a thorough overhaul. It must be three weeks since that money-grabber Doctor Anstruther went right over me, and then he had the cheek to tell me I was as fit as a fiddle when he knows perfectly well how I suffer with my head and my abdomen. Sometimes I wonder whether you doctors know anything at all or whether you just pretend with all those fancy names you don't want us to understand.' She stood up. 'Will you have me on the bed?'

I unwound my stethoscope and said 'Yes,' I would have her on the bed.

By the time I escaped from the Hon. Mrs Magnus-Wight's it was after one o'clock. I still had half my visits to do and had not had any lunch. I was grateful to Wilfred for one thing. I knew now that I would never swap one Mrs Jones, Mrs Pickle or Mrs Catterwell for ten Mrs Magnus-Wights. I was temperamentally suited to my own practice and could never stand the mumbo-jumbo of Society medicine. If my patients were suffering from a chronic complaint for which there was no known cure, I liked to explain this to them while perhaps prescribing some palliative treatment. I could never stand by and watch them pay for endless 'courses' of injections or physiotherapy at the end of which the condition remained unchanged. I was aware that this was what the private patient wanted, but there were other doctors, more suited to the task than I, very willing to provide it for them. To me a sore throat was a sore throat and could never be acute pharyngitis, no matter how much the patient was willing to pay me to tell him so.

On my way home I rang Sylvia from a call-box to see if there were any urgent calls to do or whether I could come home first for lunch. George Leech, she said, had one of his funny attacks, and could I go as soon as possible. Lunch would have to wait.

George, who had phoned me every week since trying to sell me the American convertible, with tempting offers of second-hand bargains (by some strange coincidences always owned previously by vicars or old ladies), and first-hand extravagances, was having, as I thought he would be, one of his usual attacks of pain. As I examined him I saw him watching me shiftily and knew that he was expecting me to deliver my usual lecture.

George, we had discovered by means of a sigmoidoscopy, had a slow-growing malignant tumour of his colon. He had been told, many times by me and twice by surgeons to whom I had referred him, that since it was in the early stages, the growth could be removed surgically with an extremely good prognosis. George, however, was one of those fortunately rare people with an almost pathological fear of surgery and absolutely refused to allow himself to be 'cut up.' He was impervious to pleas, threats and the most forthright account I could manage of what would happen to him if he continued to bury his head in the sand. Neither I nor the knowledge that the tumour would most certainly kill him if he delayed too long could move him. Even his occasional attacks of pain failed to persuade him.

I gave him a tablet to relieve the pain and sat down on the end of the bed to wait until it began to work.

He lay back on the pillow and looked at me from beneath his lowered eyelids. 'Well?' he said.

'Well?'

'Arencher going to say it?'

'I'm fed up with saying it, George,' I said. 'Surely your pain must remind you of what's going on inside you. Let me arrange for you to go into St Anthony's for operation. You'd be out in three weeks and there'd be no reason why you shouldn't be flogging cars thirty years from now.'

'Over my dead body, Doc.'

'It will be, George. Look, if something's wrong with a car engine you have it repaired, don't you? You don't wait until the car packs up.'

George grinned. 'That's what'll happen to your tin can if you don't watch out. Find yerself sitting in the middle of the road one day wiv no back axle. Why'nt you let 'er go, Doc? I gotta lovely silver-grey saloon, twenny-five to the gall...' His voice was becoming blurry as the tablet began to work.

'Can't afford it just now, George,' I said, and indeed with a forthcoming increase in the family I would have to start saving up. 'But it wouldn't cost you a penny to have your operation.'

He was drifting off to sleep. 'You buy a new car offa me,' he said, 'an' I'll consirrer the marrer...'

I got up and stood over the bed. 'George,' I said, 'I wish you realised that your life is in danger, not some miserable back axle. It's a different thing altogether...' He was asleep. I knew that even if he had heard it would have made no difference. He had heard it all before.

Since it was already so late I decided to stop for a cup of coffee at the 'Playfair,' then finish the rest of my visits before going home. As I walked into the restaurant, Archibald Compton was paying his bill. I wanted to ask him why he now had the Hart family on his list, but I could hardly do it in front of the cashier. We nodded to each other and I sat down. Doctor Compton finished paying his bill, then came over to where I was sitting. 'Ah!' I thought, 'he's coming to explain about the Harts.' He put a hand on my shoulder and bent towards my ear.

'Try the toad-in-the-hole, old man,' he said. 'It's awfully good.'

Nine

Since Sylvia was now about three months pregnant, I had to decide whom I was going to ask to deliver our baby. Whilst many of my patients had their babies at home, or in hospital (in the case of first babies or special cases) under the Health Scheme, there were many who preferred to pay for the more individual attention of a particular gynæcologist whom they attended privately. During the time I had been in general practice I had become on increasingly familiar terms with three or four gynæcologists, each of whom I was sure would be only too pleased to look after Sylvia. Apart from the fact that doctors were always willing to look after a colleague and his family, my choice of specialist for my wife implied a tacit agreement that I would continue to send my gynæ. cases to him. The specialist in private practice still, of course, depended upon the general practitioners for his livelihood; he could see no patient unless that patient was referred to him by a GP.

The subject of medical etiquette is a prickly one and one which often mystifies the layman. The public, by and large, understand medical ethics (professional secrecy, refusal of one doctor to treat a patient already under the care of another without permission), but many people are still baffled by the reasons underlying medical etiquette. They are quite unable to grasp why they should not go and see Dr So-and-so about their heart without all that hanky-panky (as it seems to them) of going to their own doctor before and after their visit to the specialist. They do not appreciate that the rules of etiquette are made for their own good and that it is vitally important to them that the family doctor remains in control. They view the whole procedure with suspicion as though the rules had been drawn up to protect the vested interests of the doctors, and tend to forget that if they are taken seriously ill on a Saturday night it will be the family doctor who will have to treat them and not the consultant.

Usually each GP referred his patients to one of a small group of consultants in whose ability he had faith, and as the years rolled on a letterhead romance began and blossomed. To the newly qualified GP, sending his first patients to the consultant of his choice, the opinion would return under the formal greeting: 'Dear Doctor Smith.' Many months, and a few opinions later, the courtship would advance a stage further:

'My dear Doctor Smith,' followed at not too long an interval by 'Dear Smith' and 'My dear Smith.' At this stage in the wooing, practitioner and consultant might possibly meet in order to discuss a case with the inevitable outcome: 'Dear John.' By the time 'My dear John' terms were reached the partnership was sealed and could look forward to many happy years of successful co-operation.

After nearly two years in general practice I was on first-name terms with three gynæcologists when I had to decide about our own child. I discovered that it was one thing to choose a consultant for a patient, quite another when it came to one's own family. My cool powers of decision had gone and I felt quite dithery. Since each one of the men I was considering was equally competent, obstetrically speaking, it seemed to boil down to a question of temperament. Each patient looked for something different in her gynæcologist, as she did in her GP. As a colleague of mine once said: 'I always send the weepy ones to so-and-so,' which put the whole matter in a nutshell.

Of the men I was considering asking to look after Sylvia, one was a forthright Irishman, superb at his job but who never molly-coddled a patient; one was a smooth young man who described to me in detail in his letters each loving stitch or whiff of anæsthetic he had to administer – his patients adored him; and the third was a huntin', shootin' and fishin' nobleman in his sixties who had come to the house once when I had called him out to see a patient of mine, and sat taking notes about her while I had my dinner. Unfortunately he had not at first put a book or a newspaper under the sheet on which he wrote, and we still had the legend 'Miss Baker is a virgin' imprinted in his flowing hand on the polished top of our dining-room table.

Since I had great faith in the skill of each of these men, I decided to leave the final choice to Sylvia. She did not take long to make up her mind. She liked being molly-coddled, she said, but not by old men. Together we went to see Mr Humphrey Mallow.

Put by one sympathy-exuding, crisp, white receptionist into the hands of a second sympathy-exuding, crisp, white receptionist, we were finally ushered into the vast, high-ceilinged sanctum of Mr Mallow, who, meeting us at the door, guided Sylvia like a piece of rare old china to a chair, gave me a curt nod, and went to sit behind his desk.

'Now,' he said, pen in hand, showing Sylvia a complete upper and lower set and two brown eyes loaded with compassion, 'what is the full name?'

It was no wonder they fell like ninepins under his charm. I had plenty of time to examine the beautiful room, his books, his flowers, photographs of his wife, oil-paintings of his children, while he had a heart-to-heart talk with Sylvia. When he had finished I felt sure that she, like the patients I had sent him, would be his slave for ever. He sent her with the nurse, summoned by a discreet bell, into the examination room and then, and only then, turned to me.

When the nurse told him that Sylvia was ready to be examined he excused himself and glided out. I nipped round behind his large desk to see what he had written in his notes about Sylvia. He had one full page of information noted down in his detailed and precise way. At the end of the page he had written in capital letters: BOY. It was an old dodge of gynæcologists. They wrote BOY, large and clear, in their notes and then told the patient categorically that she was going to give birth to a girl. If a girl was born all was well; the patient much impressed with his diagnostic powers; if a boy arrived, he would conveniently forget what he had told the patient and proudly produce his note made unmistakably at the time of the mother's first visit. It was a simple wangle, but either way he couldn't lose. Mr Humphrey Mallow was obviously not going to miss a trick.

I was still on the wrong side of the desk when I looked up to see the nurse, who had crept silently in on the thick-piled carpet, looking at me disapprovingly. I tried not to look like a guilty schoolboy and, putting my hands in my pockets, whistled a little, going on to examine the flowers as if I had been merely taking an inventory of the whole room.

'Mr Mallow says would you like to come and have a look at your wife,' she said.

I wanted to tell her that I had seen my wife before, but followed her large white feet out of the room.

Sylvia, partly undressed, lay on the examination couch. Mr Mallow was rubbing his hands and beaming at her.

'Everything seems fine,' he said; 'we should have no difficulties here. She seems to have about a twelve-week pregnancy. You can just feel the uterus over the brim of the pelvis.' He pushed back the towel on Sylvia's tummy and felt. He then invited me to have a feel. After I had confirmed his findings and winked at Sylvia, Mallow said: 'By the way, how did that patient of yours, Mrs Plowright, do on that testosterone I gave her?'

Mrs Plowright had an interesting gynæcological condition which had been causing her trouble for many years. I thought that Mr Mallow was at last helping her, and told him how she was progressing with the treatment he had prescribed.

'It reminds me of a very similar case I had when I was in Newcastle,' he said, and began to tell me about it. When he was only halfway through a voice from the couch said:

'Do you mind if I get dressed now?'

We both looked at Sylvia. Mallow was instantly all contrition.

'My dear girl,' he said, 'how stupid of us.' He smiled at her disarmingly. 'You know how it is when we start talking "shop."'

'Yes,' Sylvia said resignedly, she knew how it was.

While Sylvia got dressed I went back with Mallow to the consulting-room. Sitting at his desk he made notes on his findings by examination.

'Everything all right?' I said casually, more to make conversation than anything else.

I was surprised when he didn't answer immediately.

'I'm not very happy about her blood pressure,' he said, stroking his chin. 'The diastolic was a hundred and ten. We shall have to keep an eye on her.'

I felt depressed. Although there was no immediate danger, if Sylvia should turn out to have high blood pressure it was a worrying condition which could lead to complications, and she would have to be very carefully watched.

'Cheer up,' Mallow said. 'I've delivered many doctors' wives, and they all seem to develop some peculiarity or other with which to plague their husbands. The best thing is to let me do the worrying. I'll look after Sylvia.'

He was kind, but I was still upset. We decided not to say anything about her raised blood pressure to Sylvia, but that I was to watch her and make sure she did not tire herself.

Outside on the marble, pillar-surrounded step I asked Sylvia how she had liked Mr Mallow.

'I think he's charming,' she said. 'But next time, if you don't mind, I shall go alone.'

'Why?' I asked, hopping nimbly round to walk on the outside of the pavement.

'Because I don't like lying there as if I was in the cattle market while you two discuss my attributes.'

I laughed. 'You'll get used to it,' I said airily; 'all doctors' wives do. Anyway, he says you're going to have a lovely baby.'

'A girl,' Sylvia said. 'I hope he's right. Little girls are adorable.'

I didn't tell her about the 'BOY' Mallow had written in her notes, nor that I rather fancied a boy myself. She was in rather a touchy mood these days and there was no point in upsetting her. Anyway, we would, I hoped, have more than one child, and would ultimately both get what we wanted.

Driving home we made a provisional date for our dinner party at which we were to introduce Faraday to Tessa Brindley, and discussed the menu and guest list. We dismissed half our friends as too dull, too stuffy or too old to provide a light-hearted setting for the romance we were hoping to bring about, and finally decided upon Sylvia's friend Molly, for colour, and her new, long-haired artist boyfriend, for intellect. The party was to be completed by my old friend Loveday, the dentist, and his wife, who were always excellent conversationalists and good mixers.

The food problem was not so easily resolved, because at every suggestion I made Sylvia said she felt sick. She had been suffering from nausea for the past few weeks, and said that if she didn't feel any better by the night of the party she would just have to sit in the kitchen with her tea and toast while we tucked into our roast duck or tournedos or whatever other cannibal-like dish we decided on. On second thoughts, she said, we should probably all be drinking tea and eating toast because she couldn't even bear to cook anything fit for a dinner party, and the most Iris could rise to was the frying pan, out of which she and I were at present living.

I promised her that in another couple of weeks her nausea would have disappeared completely and that she would most probably be thinking of nothing but food and eating – as my pregnant patients assured me they were – 'enough for two.' We decided to leave the menu until a later date.

As we drew up outside the house I saw Iris' burning bush of hair pushing aside the dining-room curtain. She came bouncing out of the house to meet us.

'Oh! Doctor,' she said, 'I've got a man in the waiting-room with his neck all like this.' She twisted her head until it was grossly contorted. 'He's in terrible pain, but I sat him down and said you'd be sure to be able to put it right.' Iris had implicit faith in my healing powers. 'I'll get your case,' she said, and made for the car.

'I shan't need that, Iris,' I said. 'Go and tell

him I'll be with him in a few minutes.'

Mr Westbeech, our good-looking local librarian, had a cervical disc lesion and was, as Iris had said, in severe pain.

I decided to try and manipulate it for him and told him to lie on the couch with his head at the foot end. Getting into position behind his head, I asked him to hold on tightly to the sides of the couch while I pulled his head. It was no good. Every time I pulled, his hands slipped against the leather of the couch and he slid towards me. I needed someone to assist me by holding his shoulders. Asking Mr Westbeech to lie still for a moment, I went to find Sylvia.

In the kitchen Iris and Sylvia were sitting with cups of tea talking, as they usually were, babies. I told Sylvia what I wanted her to do, and she got up. Coming round the table, Iris pushed her gently back into the chair and looked at me disgustedly.

'You can't let her come into the surgery and pull and push,' she said vehemently. 'What about the baby?' She untied her apron. 'I'll come and help you.'

Iris, of course, was right. I had completely forgotten about the baby. In the hall Iris stood on her toes to look in the mirror and pat her hair.

'Come on,' I said impatiently, 'you're only going to hold his shoulders for me, not dance with him.'

Iris giggled.

I explained to Mr Westbeech that Iris would sit on the side of the couch and pull his shoulders as hard as she could towards her while I, from the foot of the couch, would try again to pull his head towards me. If I could manage to get his neck extended sufficiently, his disc should slip gently back into position.

Iris wriggled herself into place on the couch and took a grim hold on the broad shoulders of the suffering Mr Westbeech. Gently but firmly I began to pull his head towards me with both hands. I was red in the face with exertion and Iris was tugging with all her might. Between the two of us Mr Westbeech closed his eyes and hoped for the best. The neck was still not fully extended. I pulled a little harder: Iris, unable to pull as hard as I, lost her grip and fell into the arms of Mr Westbeech, who yelled with pain as his neck retracted into its former painful position.

'Oh! Iris!' I said reproachfully, although it hadn't been her fault, poor girl. She reddened and lifted her head off Mr Westbeech's camel-haired waistcoat.

'Sorry,' she said.

Mr Westbeech sighed.

'Sorry, old man,' I said; 'we'll try again once more. If we don't manage it this time I'll have to send you to the orthopædic hospital. They've a special harness there for this job.'

Sweating from the exertion, I took off my jacket and rolled up my sleeves. Iris sat down again on the couch and Mr Westbeech clenched his fists.

'Right,' I said to Iris. 'Pull!'

The second hand of the wall clock slid silently round. My forehead was damp, Iris was pale with determination not to lose her grip, and Mr Westbeech was moaning softly. Suddenly there was a 'click.' The disc, I hoped, had returned to its normal position. Very slowly I released the tension on his neck. Iris sat up and pushed back the hair from her eyes. I told Mr Westbeech to rest for a moment and then, very carefully, try to sit up. By the time I had my jacket on he was sitting up and turning his head gingerly from side to side.

'It's gone!' he said disbelievingly. 'It's absolutely gone! That's terrific, Doctor. It was so painful. I just reached up to a high shelf to get a book and I couldn't turn my head back again.' He sat there rubbing his neck and flexing it.

'You should be all right now,' I said; 'but this condition does recur occasionally once it's happened. Try to avoid any sudden head movements for a day or two until it's had a chance to settle down.'

He stood up. 'Thanks again, Doctor. I will.'

He turned to Iris and grinned. 'Thanks for

your help.'

'Not at all.' Irish blushed. 'Sorry for squashing you.'

'It would have been a great pleasure at any other time.'

I thought it was time I brought the interview to an end, and opened the door.

Iris darted forward and picked two long red hairs from Mr Westbeech's waistcoat.

'Your wife might not believe where they came from,' she said.

Mr Westbeech winked at her. 'I'm not married,' he said; 'but thanks all the same.'

Ten

Faraday, Tessa Brindley, the Lovedays, Molly and her boyfriend all said they would be delighted to come to dinner with us. Sylvia was no longer feeling ill at the sight or mention of food and we had decided on the menu. It was to be nothing too ambitious, as Humphrey Mallow had come to the conclusion that Sylvia did have essential hypertension and that it was important for her to get as much rest as possible. We had told her that it was necessary for her to take care, and she was cheerfully co-operative.

At breakfast-time on the day before the

dinner party Sylvia said: 'I hope you're going to get your hair cut before tomorrow.'

'Impossible,' I said. 'I haven't a moment today, and tomorrow is early closing. It'll have to wait until next week.' I put my mind back to the letter I was reading about a patient.

'Go somewhere where it isn't early closing,' Sylvia said.

I looked at her in surprise. 'Don't be ridiculous. Bob Flower's been cutting my hair ever since I came here. I couldn't possibly go anywhere else, any more than he would consult another doctor. Bob would be most offended. In addition to which, I haven't got the time.' I picked up the letter again. 'Anyway, I only had it cut last week,' I said finally.

'Last month, you mean. Sweetie, you can't possibly look like that for tomorrow. Not when you're the host. You'll just have to find a moment.'

'They're not going to eat *me*,' I said. 'And whatever I look like, Faraday's seen me far worse and, for that matter, so have the Lovedays. Before I was married I hardly ever used to get my hair cut at all; I always forgot. As for Tessa Brindley, she's not coming here to look at me, so I really can't see that it matters all that much.'

'Well, it matters to me,' Sylvia said, tears in her voice. 'I don't want my husband sitting at the top of the table with hair down to his shoulders.'

I sighed. 'Don't exaggerate, darling. It's not as bad as all that!'

'It's worse,' Sylvia said.

As her pregnancy advanced and I watched Sylvia becoming more and more emotional and excited over trifles, I realised I was now getting first-hand experience of what I had previously only heard in the surgery. 'My wife's impossible, Doctor,' the expectant fathers would tell me. 'She gets upset at everything and turns on the taps at the slightest possible excuse. Is that normal?' 'Absolutely,' I'd say airily. 'You must understand that women are emotionally disturbed at this time. You must just be extra patient and extra kind, and try not to upset her.'

'You will make time, won't you, Sweetie?' Sylvia pleaded, and I felt the glib words I had handed out so casually to patients blow back in my face. 'She's emotionally disturbed,' I told myself, 'and you must be a little extra kind.' I was so rushed that I didn't see how I could possibly take an hour off in the middle of the afternoon to get my hair cut.

'I'll try,' I said, and saw her face clear. 'I'll really try.'

Iris put her head round the door.

'Doctor,' she said, 'it's nearly ten past nine

and the waiting-room is packed. I think you'd better start. There's already six visits on the list and you'll never get through.'

I grinned at Sylvia. Whatever misdemeanour I committed, I could always defend myself with Iris. Since I had brought her back with me from Edinburgh she had more than made up for Bridget and Emily, and was worth twice as much as we paid her.

She was always cheerful and unafraid of work, and took a personal interest in the house and practice. Her faults were bearable. She was inclined to be too 'matey,' frequently walking into the bedroom without knocking, and cheerfully giving her unsolicited advice when Sylvia and I were discussing something when she was within earshot, and she often took it upon herself to diagnose and prescribe for the patients rather than disturb me. I was tired of telling her that she mustn't give advice off her own bat, but all she'd do was grin and say: 'I wouldn't dream of bothering you with some of the things they phone up for.' I had already caught her prescribing porridge for a swallowed farthing, hot milk and whisky for a cold, and a bread poultice for what turned out to be mumps. Iris was quite unrepentant and said if she had her way she could cut down my visits by half.

To Sylvia she was indispensable, dancing round her all day in case she lifted something that was too heavy, and insisting that she put her feet up whenever she could. For all this Sylvia could forgive her for the raids on her nail-varnish and the fact that when we went out Iris tried on every garment in her wardrobe and put them back none too tidily. We had both grown fond of her and hoped that her itchy feet would not lure her away too soon. She had promised, at any rate, to stay until the baby was born.

I hadn't been kidding Sylvia about not having time to get my hair cut. The practice had suddenly got very busy and I seemed to have a lot of really ill people on my hands all at once. It was difficult to make up my mind which visit to do first. I hesitated between a small child with severe stomach pains accompanied by vomiting and a high temperature, and an old man who seemed to his wife to be extremely ill. I decided to have a look at the child first.

I was just driving away from the house, having prescribed for the child and reassured the mother that there was no acute surgical emergency, when I heard a bicycle bell pealing urgently and coming nearer. Looking in the mirror I saw a red-haired girl on a bike pedalling furiously towards me and waving one arm in the air. I stopped and stuck my head out of the window as Iris drew up. Her skirt was above her knees, she was out of breath, and her face was nearly as red as her hair.

'Thank goodness I caught you,' she said, panting to regain her breath. 'I thought you'd be doing the stomach pains first, so I took a chance.'

'What's the matter?'

'Mr Johnson, 55 Buckhurst, just came round with his lorry,' she gasped. 'He says that Mr Melrose hasn't gone to work this morning and the children haven't gone to school. He went next door to see what was the matter, but there was no reply. He couldn't open the door, all the windows were shut up tight, and there was a smell of gas coming from the letter box. I think you'd better hurry.'

I revved up. 'I will,' I said. 'Thanks, Iris.' The rest of the calls would just have to wait a little.

Outside fifty-seven Buckhurst Crescent a police car and a fire engine had already drawn up, summoned, no doubt, by the neighbours, who stood in a little headscarfed group round the front door.

A fireman with a mask round his face was breaking in the front door. The neighbours, sharp eyes in apprehensive faces, watched him silently. The milkman, drawing up in his electric-motored float, got out, whistling, two pint bottles under his arm.

'Wassermarrer?'

'Dunno...'

'Never went to work this morning...'
'Kids never went to school...'
'Smell o' gas...'

The milkman, now in the picture, stayed to watch, the bottles still under his arm.

The door open, the little group pushed noisily forward to peer into the dark passage. The police officer put out an official arm and told them to stand back.

I stood on the dirty red step waiting until the masked fireman who had gone in gave the all-clear.

I could not help feeling apprehensive. Mr Melrose had lost his wife a year ago. She had died from disseminated sclerosis, a progressive disease through which her husband, with the help of the neighbours, had nursed her throughout her last bedridden months.

Since her death Melrose, a little, harassed man in his early forties, had run the house by himself and looked after the eight-year-old twin girls. I had seen him in the surgery a few weeks ago, when he had consulted me about his headaches and he had told me that he was worried about losing his job. He was a panel-beater in a factory, and there had been rumours that some of the workers might be laid off during the summer months. Standing obediently on the step, waiting for the all-clear from the fireman, I hoped that his responsibilities had not proved too much for the quiet, overburdened little man.

‘OK, Doc!’ a voice yelled from upstairs. ‘Put yer ’ankerchief rahnd yer fice.’

I did as I was told and followed the police officer up the carpetless stairs.

In the front room, fully clothed on the large double bed, lay Mr Melrose, blue-faced and looking smaller than ever. On either side of him, but in their nightclothes, beneath greyish blankets, the twins seemingly slept. The gas fire, now innocently silent, had, the fireman told us, been hissing steadily, full on. Together we lifted Mr Melrose on to the floor and pulled back the blankets to look at the little girls. Mr Melrose was alive, but only just; I doubted whether it was possible to save him. One little girl was still breathing faintly, but her sister appeared to be dead.

I started artificial respiration on Mr Melrose and instructed the police officer and the fireman to do the same to the little girls while we waited for the ambulance.

By the time it came it was obvious that nothing could be done for the little girl who was dead, and it seemed unlikely that the other one would survive. Mr Melrose, however, on whom I had been working, seemed to be breathing a little better and I thought that he might have a faint chance. The ambulance men now undertook to keep up the rhythmic resuscitative movement on Mr Melrose and the one child all the way to the hospital.

We carried them out past the women huddled on the front path and into the ambulance which, with its anxious bell, had drawn more women on to their doorsteps and others to their windows. They watched it drive quickly down the road, and not until it had turned the corner did their tongues loosen.

'Might 'ave bin an accident...'

'Them poor kids...'

'Was 'e dead?...'

'Look, there was paper in the winders...'

'Puts me in mind of my Sydney when they took him away.'

The milkman, still clutching his two bottles under his arms, went his way, his whistle forgotten, his face sad.

I went back into the house for my case. In the bedroom, now blown through with clean air from the open windows, the policeman was filling his small book with meticulous notes.

'What a bloody thing to do!' he said, looking at the rumpled, grubby bed.

'It wasn't accidental, then?'

He picked up the strips of newspaper which Melrose had stuffed under the door.

'Doesn't look like it.' He wrote something down. 'I've got a kid that age myself. What's he like – Melrose?'

'Just an ordinary sort of chap,' I said. 'His

wife died. Perhaps he found life too much.'

'Perhaps he did. But to try to get rid of the youngsters...'

There was nothing more I could do. I left him measuring up and making notes and went off to finish my visits. It was difficult to remove from my mind the image of Mr Melrose and his two little girls, lying silently on the sad-looking bed.

The day progressed badly. The old man, whose wife had thought he looked extremely ill, turned out to have pneumonia; Mrs Douthwaite had a sudden hæmoptysis, and I had to hang on the phone for over half an hour trying to get her admitted to hospital. At five o'clock I got the news that both the little Melrose girls were dead but that Melrose himself looked as if he would recover. When I considered the future the poor man had now to face I could feel no elation at the thought that I had probably saved his life.

Without having had a moment to relax all day, I began the evening surgery. An hour after my normal closing time I buzzed for the last patient. It was Bob Flower. At the sight of him I put a guilty hand to the long hair crawling down my neck.

'Hallo, Bob,' I said. 'I should have been in to get my hair cut this week, but I haven't had a moment.'

'I know,' Bob said. 'I met your wife at

lunch-time in the High Street.'

'Sit down,' I said, stamping the date on a prescription pad – Bob usually needed a fresh prescription for his asthma tablets – 'and tell me what the trouble is.'

He remained standing. 'No trouble,' he said, and, reaching into his pockets, took out a comb and two pairs of scissors and put them on my desk.

'What on earth are you doing, Bob?'

He went over to the basin and took a clean towel from where he knew I kept them, in the cupboard underneath. Coming towards me, he put it round my shoulders. 'Cutting your hair,' he said, and picked up the scissors and comb. 'If Mohammed won't come to the mountain...'

I sat back relaxed. 'All right, Bob,' I said. 'Carry on.'

'You want to make some money tomorrow?' he asked, snipping skilfully. 'Rose Marie in the three-thirty. One of my regulars gave it to me...'

It was not unpleasant to sit in the surgery and listen to somebody else doing the talking.

It had been a hectic day. Sylvia, against my better judgement, persuaded me to go to bed half an hour earlier than usual.

'I hate doing this,' I grumbled as I took my shirt off, 'because whenever I decide to go to bed early I have to get out again. It's always best to wait until most of the patients have gone to bed, then you know that they won't suddenly discover that little Johnny is breathing heavily, or swallow a fish bone while they're having a late snack.'

Sylvia laughed. 'I'm sure they won't this evening,' she said. 'There seems to be nothing else that can happen.'

But there was. I had just switched off the light, opened the curtains, opened the window, tripped over the waste-paper basket and got one leg between the sheets when the phone rang. When I'd taken the message I took my leg out of bed, tripped over the waste-paper basket, closed the window, closed the curtains, switched on the light and took out my night-call pullover. 'I must remember to put a bulb in the bedside lamp,' I said to Sylvia, but she had hidden her head beneath the bedclothes with shame. 'Shan't be long,' I said, patting the mound that she made in the covers; 'don't go to sleep.'

When I came back half an hour later, Sylvia was sitting up reading the *British Medical Journal*.

'Was it necessary?'

'It depends what you mean,' I said, undressing for the second time. 'It was Mr Daly; you know, the chap with the big fat wife who always walks past here with that shopping basket on wheels. He came home from business, fit as a fiddle, went upstairs to undress and collapsed on the floor. He was dead when I got there. Only forty-five.'

'Oh! no!' Sylvia put down the *BMJ*. 'How dreadful. What was the matter with him?'

'Possibly a coronary,' I said, 'or a cerebral hæmorrhage. It doesn't much matter, does it? Have to have a PM in the morning.'

After I had put out the light and got into bed I held out my arms for Sylvia. Her face was wet with tears.

'What is it, darling?'

'It all seems so sad,' she said. 'That poor Mrs Daly! One minute she has a husband and the next she's all alone. One day she's trotting happily by with that ridiculous basket thing and the next she's crying for her husband.'

'That's life,' I said. 'We can't live for ever.'

'Not for ever, but he was only forty-five. I never realised life could be like this before I married you. When I was modelling all we used to think about was clothes; we never worried about what went on underneath them. It reminds me of a ball game I used to play as a child. You had three chances and if you were hit you were first sick, then dying, then dead. Mr Daly didn't even get his first two chances. Doesn't it depress you, Sweetie?'

'It used to,' I said, drying her tears with my handkerchief, 'but I can't cry over every man, woman and child. It's not that I don't care, but that I believe there's a reason for it all. There has to be.'

I wasn't sorry that the day which had brought tragedy to the Melrose family and Mrs Daly had ended.

Eleven

On the morning of the party, standing in front of my shaving mirror, I discovered with a small shock that I was beginning to look like a typical GP. Possibly it was the first time for many months that I had really looked at my face in a detached sort of way. I had usually been too intent on making the customary shaving grimaces in order to reach the farthest portions of my beard to see more than a small portion of myself at any one time.

Bearing in mind the evening's entertainment, however, I had allowed myself a little longer than usual for shaving, and when the job was finished had stood back a little to admire my handiwork. I wasn't going to have Sylvia saying 'Aren't you going to run over your face, Sweetie?' ten minutes before the guests arrived. It wasn't that I had got fat, although I had, it was true, a more solid appearance than I had a year ago. I had got what I can only call a benevolent, married look; a settled down, family man appearance.

I wondered if the patients had noticed it, and felt that they most probably had. At any rate, since I had been married many of my women patients had brought to me the problems which before they had taken to some older practitioner with a wife and family rather than consult a bachelor about their personal problems. Recently the picture had changed, and I could not blame the women for their former reluctance to bring to me non-medical problems which before I could not properly have understood. Now I had some experience from the other side of the fence, and had seen for myself some of the 'kitchen sink' troubles with which women had to cope. Now I was also beginning to see the trials and tribulations of pregnancy, my previous experience having been only of the purely medical aspects. I supposed that not until I actually had my own children would I be accepted as the complete family doctor. I had diagnosed measles and treated infected ears, but I still had never had to deal with a child of my own who screamed for apparently no reason in the middle of the night, or who refused to take its feeds. I had that pleasure to come, but knew that when it did I should be able to bring just that much more sympathy and understanding to mothers with similar problems.

The surgery was again packed, and at the end of my visiting list was an address I was unable to read. It was '3' something or other, but I couldn't make out the name of the road. It was in Sylvia's writing. She was in the kitchen stirring something over a saucepan of boiling water.

'What is it?' she said. 'I can't stop or the sauce will curdle.'

'Never mind that. I can't read one of my calls.' I stuck the paper under her nose and pointed to the last line.

'Oh!' she said. 'Three bottles of Château Neuf du Pape! The wine; for tonight. You won't forget, will you?'

'I'll try not to. I'm frightfully busy, though.'

'Did you leave Mrs Waddell's prescription?'

'Yes.'

'And remember Mr Glynn's ambulance? He has to be at the Orthopædic at three.'

'No. I'll do that now.' I kissed the back of her neck. 'I don't know how I ever managed without you.'

'It's thickened!' she shouted joyfully, dripping some yellow stuff off the wooden spoon, and I could see that today her mind wasn't really on the practice.

Sylvia very nearly didn't get to her own

dinner party either. At seven o'clock, having worked hard all day, she had completed all the preparations. The table was laid, with all our wedding-present finery, the house tidy and the dinner practically ready to be served. I was in the bathroom 'running over my face' at Sylvia's request, when the doorbell rang.

'I'll go,' Sylvia said. 'Iris is changing her apron. It's too early for visitors, anyway.'

I heard her open the front door, and an exchange of voices. Then there seemed to be a long silence. Just as I came out on to the landing to see what was going on a woman's voice shouted:

'Oy! Is anybody there?'

I leaned over the banisters. 'Yes?'

'Oh! it's you, Doctor. You'd better come down. I think your wife's took queer.'

Sylvia was sitting with her head in her hands on the bottom stair.

On the doorstep, clutching something in her hands, stood Mrs Bradshaw from the Council estate.

'What happened?' I said.

'I'm ever so sorry, but I must've upset 'er. It's my daughter what was expecting and started losin' 'eavy this morning. You know you told me to keep it if anything seemed to come away, so I thought I'd save you the trouble of coming round.' She held up the glass jam jar she had been holding so carefully. In it, in a quantity of blood, was a three-months fœtus!

I got rid of the well-meaning Mrs Bradshaw and sat on the step next to Sylvia.

'Come on, Sweetie,' I said; 'you're a doctor's wife.'

'I'm sorry,' she said, leaning against me. 'It gave me rather a shock for the moment. I opened the door and she just thrust the wretched thing under my nose. It's made me feel a bit odd.'

I helped her up the stairs and told her to lie down for a bit until she felt better. I promised to come up as soon as anyone arrived.

In the drawing-room, Faraday was sampling the drinks and warming his backside in front of the electric fire.

'I didn't hear you ring,' I said.

'I didn't. I came round the back. I thought Sylvia would be in the kitchen, but all I could see was a mass of vital statistics with red hair. She gave me one of these because I hadn't had any tea.' He held out the *petit four* he was eating.

I explained what had happened to Sylvia.

'Does she need a doctor?' Faraday said, helping himself to another drink. 'A proper doctor?'

'No. And if you don't put that whisky bottle down you'll be maudlin before anyone comes. I hope you haven't forgotten that this dinner party is entirely for your benefit.'

'My dear fellow,' Faraday drained his glass and smacked his lips appreciatively, 'of course I haven't. That's why I'm giving myself moral support.' He wandered round the room, then arranged himself carefully on the arm of the chair facing the door.

'How do I look?' he asked. 'Appetising?'

'Tessa might think so,' I said.

'I think this will do nicely,' Faraday said, patting the chair. 'It's the first meeting of the eye that's so important.'

'Sylvia's made a plan,' I said. 'In case you want to talk to Tessa alone she's borrowed Molly's record player and I've fixed it up in the morning-room.'

Faraday raised an eyebrow. 'The etchings routine?'

'Yes,' I said, 'only it's skiffle or rock and roll.'

'Sylvia's thought of everything.'

'She says it's difficult to perform these introductions at private dinner parties. It's better at a dance, where you can wander off on your own.'

'Don't worry,' Faraday said. 'If Tessa's everything you say, just leave it to me.'

The bell rang and Faraday carefully arranged his face into what he considered was a charming smile. It was Loveday and his wife. Iris, bouncing perkily in, showed them into the room. Faraday breathed a small sigh of relief and got up to meet them.

Having made the introduction, I went to fetch Sylvia. She was coming down the stairs, a little pale, but feeling better.

'Fix my safety pin,' she whispered, and held up the bottom of her evening jumper.

I fastened the large pin in the waistband of her skirt, which now, in the sixteenth week of her pregnancy, she was unable to do up, and she pulled the black jumper neatly over the rift. She kissed her thanks and we went to make ourselves sociable.

Loveday and his wife were the ideal guests. Loveday, fat, jolly, and ruddy-faced from the golf course, stood by the mantelpiece rubbing his hands, laughing noisily and keeping up a witty flow of interesting small talk. Mrs Loveday, when she could get a word in sideways, as always put everyone at ease with her quiet manner and her genuine interest in the people she met.

Molly and her friend were the next to arrive, and when I had got over my momentary shock at his appearance I went forward to make the introductions. The boyfriend, Eric, was wearing a raspberry-coloured shirt, a green tie, and sandals. He pushed the hair out of his intellectual eyes, told Sylvia how frightfully kind it was of her to ask him to dinner, and sat on the floor. He accepted a glass of sherry with great intensity and said, 'What do you think about Dufy?' tossing the remark like a ball to the room at large.

Into the silence that followed, Molly, in her Glynis Johns mood, said huskily to Mrs Loveday: 'Eric's an artist.'

'I would never have guessed,' Mrs Loveday said in her quiet, charming way. 'As for Dufy, while no one can deny his superb draughtsmanship, he was far too much of the fantasist for my liking.'

Eric, surprised to have his ball picked up and returned, shuffled along the floor until he was sitting at her feet.

'But that's the whole point,' he said. 'He wanted to give a kind of fairytale glamour to contemporary life. His art is a precious concentrate of French life, a sort of civilised hedonism, don't you think?'

Mrs Loveday didn't think, but proceeded to cross swords with Eric in a ladylike, debunking manner. I kept an eye on them while talking golf with Loveday, and was pleased to see that Mrs Loveday was more than holding her own.

They had finished with Dufy and returned to Cézanne and the Cubists, Faraday was on his sixth whisky, and Sylvia was looking anxiously at the clock when we heard the doorbell ring.

Sylvia went out to meet Tessa, Faraday took up his rehearsed position on the arm of the chair, and I said brightly: 'Ah! Our last guest.'

She came in in front of Sylvia and stood

for a moment shyly in the doorway. Faraday nearly fell off the arm of the chair, Loveday straightened his tie and Eric unwound himself from Mrs Loveday's feet. I had seen Tessa once or twice before, but even I felt the hard-hitting impact of her beauty.

She wasn't very tall, but what there was of her was perfect. Her figure was obtrusive without being flamboyant, her legs, sheer poetry, her hair silver-blonde and her eyes a curious, luminous green, from which, once you had met them, it was difficult to look away. In her black dress, quite plain except for a fabulously expensive-looking six-row pearl collar, she really was something quite exceptional. I wasn't surprised that her father was worried about her.

'I'm sorry I'm late,' she said to me, just nervously enough to remind one she was only eighteen. 'I had to wait for the car.'

When she had been introduced she sat down, and I looked to see how Faraday was taking it and what had happened to 'the first meeting of the eyes.' He had gone quite pale and was standing, tongue-tied, staring at her while she talked quietly to Mrs Loveday. Molly was trying to talk to Eric, but he was staring spellbound at Tessa, and Loveday whispered to me, mopping his permanently wet forehead, that he wished he was twenty-one again and single.

The dinner went off beautifully. Sylvia had

excelled herself and her cooking was appreciated by everyone except Faraday, who didn't eat a thing because he couldn't take his eyes off Tessa. I couldn't blame him. At eighteen she seemed to have everything, revealing at the dinner table a live personality which, with her looks, she could well have managed without.

Iris, in a tiny, frilly apron, nipped smartly in and out with the dishes, only forgetting herself on one occasion when she was unable to stop herself joining in the general conversation. When she realised what she had done she blushed bright red, winked at me and hastily took out her loaded tray, holding the door open with her behind.

Back in the drawing-room after dinner, Eric sat on the arm of Tessa's chair and, with one hand behind her head, from where he now and again touched her hair, questioned her about the paintings she had seen in Rome where she had recently been on holiday.

Molly, Mr and Mrs Loveday, Sylvia and I discussed the theatre, and Faraday wandered around like a caged lion, glaring at Tessa and Eric.

After about half an hour, during which only the conversation in our little group had changed, Faraday could stand it no longer. I got up and stood beside him, leaning against the mantelpiece.

'What the hell am I to do?' he whispered. 'She hasn't even noticed my existence.'

'What happened to the first meeting of the eyes?'

'I drowned.'

'Why don't you break up the tête-à-tête?' I nodded towards Tessa and Eric.

'I've tried. I can't get them out of the Sistine Chapel.'

'It'll have to be etchings then,' I said. 'Leave it to me.'

I caught Sylvia's eye and said loudly: 'Has anyone heard the latest Tommy Steele record?'

Eric winced. 'Oh!' he said. 'Rock and roll? Personally, I think it's an expression of decadence...'

'Your father told me you were one of his fans, Tessa,' I said, ignoring the interruption.

Eric realised his mistake. 'Of course, I was only quoting...' He looked frantically at Tessa. 'My own opinion...'

'Dr Faraday has a wonderful rock and roll collection,' I went on ruthlessly. 'He brought some of them with him.' I looked at Tessa. 'Perhaps you'd like to hear them in the morning-room.'

Tessa, who could not, after all, politely refuse, got up. Eric danced round to her other side as she walked with Faraday to the door. He obviously had every intention of going with them.

'Oh! Eric,' Sylvia said, and I looked at her gratefully. 'Molly was telling me that you did portraits privately. Now, I have a very good friend who is dying to have her portrait painted. Come and tell me about it.'

Eric hesitated, then seemed to remember that Sylvia, was, after all, his hostess. He closed the door reluctantly after Tessa and Faraday, and came truculently across the room.

For a while we talked against a faint background of rock and roll. Loveday entertained us with some of his stories and Eric sat in a corner sulking.

After a time I became aware that there were no longer any sounds of music filtering through from the morning-room. Sylvia had noticed it, too, and we exchanged a smile. Half an hour later we were getting anxious.

'Sweetie,' Sylvia said meaningly, 'can you come and help me get a new bottle of whisky down? I'm sure Mr Loveday can do with a nightcap.'

Outside in the hall I held Sylvia's hand and listened. There were no sounds from the morning-room.

'We'd better go and see what's happening,' I said. 'After all, Tessa is our guest and I feel a little bit responsible. You know, your friend Faraday sometimes gets a bit carried away.'

I opened the door and two guilty faces spun round towards me. Faraday and Iris were standing together in front of the fire. I wasn't sure whether or not his hands had been round her waist.

'Iris had a pain,' Faraday said nonchalantly.

'Really?' I said.

Iris blushed and sidled past me, muttering something about the washing-up.

'Where's Tessa?' Sylvia asked.

'She asked me to make her excuses to you and to say good night and thank you. She was rather embarrassed to come in and explain in front of everybody, but she had a bad headache. I said it would be all right.'

I looked at Faraday. 'Is that the truth or did you frighten her away?'

Faraday sighed. 'Unfortunately, I didn't get a chance. We simply weren't on the same wavelength. As for the rock and roll, she couldn't have cared less. She said that was just her father's idea of what her generation liked. She wouldn't even let me run her home. Said she wanted to walk, alone!' He lit a cigarette. 'Pity. It'll take me a long time to forget that girl. I shall have to brush up my technique.'

'Is that what you were doing with Iris?'

'I told you. Iris had a pain.'

'Well,' I said, 'kindly remember that she's registered with me.'

In bed, Sylvia and I discussed the evening and Tessa's odd behaviour.

'I felt all the time she wasn't really interested in any of us,' Sylvia said.

'Well, we did our best. It just didn't take. It was a nice party, anyway. Now let's go to sleep.'

We were just drifting off when the telephone rang harshly in my ear.

'Yes?' I said, taking off the receiver and praying I wouldn't have to go out.

'Doctor? It's H H Brindley here. Me and the wife were worrying over our Tessa.'

'Tessa?' I said. 'What's the matter with her?'

'Nowt's the matter,' he said. 'I was wondering when she was coming home.'

'But isn't she in?'

'No. We're sitting up.'

'I'm sorry,' I said, 'but she left here soon after ten. She said she had a headache. She was offered a lift home, but she said she'd rather walk by herself.'

'Well, she's not come in.'

I felt worried because Faraday hadn't insisted on taking her home.

'Did she say she was coming straight home?' HH asked.

'I'm afraid I don't know,' I said.

There was a silence at the other end of the phone.

'Well, maybe she met up with some of her friends,' HH said unconvincingly. 'Sorry to have troubled you, but me and the wife were waiting up, like, to see what she had to say about this pal of yours. I dare say she won't be long. Coffee bars close at midnight.'

'Let me know if I can do anything,' I said vaguely.

'Right. Thanks, Doctor. Goodnight.'

'Goodnight,' I said, and put the phone down.

We lay awake wondering what had happened to Tessa and feeling a little responsible.

Twelve

I intended phoning H H Brindley before I started the surgery to see if Tessa had got safely home. I had wakened on and off in the night, worrying about her and wondering what could possibly have happened. When I was still in the bath, though, an urgent message came from one of the patients on the Council estate, who wanted me to go round right away as 'something terrible' had happened to the baby.

'Ask what seems to be the matter,' I shouted at Iris, who had yelled the message to me after battering on the bathroom door as if the house was on fire.

'I can't,' she said. 'It was a small boy gave the message, and he's gone. He just said to hurry and was out of breath from running.'

I hurried. Mrs Padwick was a nice woman and one of the more sensible mothers who never sent for me for nothing. This morning she opened the door to me with terror and panic in her eyes.

'Doctor!' she said, before I had a chance to speak. 'I went in to the baby just after Sid left to work and he's lying there, not moving, not breathing. I think he's died!'

She ran up the stairs and I followed her.

The eighteen-months-old Padwick baby was dead.

'I'm sorry,' I said inadequately. 'Was he all right last night?'

'He did have a bit of a snuffle. But he was fine in himself.'

'There will have to be a post-mortem so that we can see what happened. My own guess is that he died from a sudden severe form of pneumonia. It does happen sometimes as quickly as that.'

'But I can't believe it.' She stroked the child as though willing him to wake. 'What will Sid say? I don't know how to tell him.'

I left her in the care of a neighbour and hurried home, promising that I would make all the necessary arrangements.

'What was it?' Sylvia asked, insisting that I at least drink my coffee before starting the surgery.

I was just about to tell her when I looked up and saw her standing there beginning to look more beautiful than ever but now in a softer, maternal way, and changed my mind, not wanting to upset her.

'Nothing much,' I said. 'Panic for nothing.'

'Don't ever lie to me,' she said. 'Apart from anything else, you're such a rotten liar.' She kissed the top of my head.

'What happened to the Padwick baby?'

'It died, for no apparent reason, in the night.'

'Oh!'

Her hands tightened for a moment on my shoulders, then she said:

'How old was it?'

'Eighteen months. A sudden pneumonia, I should imagine. It sometimes happens like that in babies.'

She started clearing the table. 'We've got chops for lunch,' she said, 'done your favourite way. Try not to be too late.' She was making a visible effort, but her voice was higher than usual and I could see that her mind was not on the chops at all but on the Padwick baby.

I got up to start the surgery but put my arms round her for a brief moment.

'You only have to sound a bit fiercer on the telephone,' I said, 'and you'll be a proper, fully fledged, heartless doctor's wife.'

My first patient was a young girl with mousy hair who looked vaguely familiar but whom I couldn't quite place. I asked her name, but she just looked down at the floor and simpered.

'Now, come along,' I said, 'I've a packed waiting-room this morning; don't let's waste any more time. What's your name?'

She giggled. 'Come off it,' she said.

'I beg your pardon?'

'Actin' like you don't know my name! You don't have to be like that. Not when there's only the two of us here.'

Light was beginning to dawn.

'Renee,' I said. 'Renee Trotter?'

'Go on,' she said; 'as if you didn't know.'

'I'm glad you came, Miss Trotter,' I said. 'I've been wanting to have a word with you. You've got to stop writing those letters to me.'

'Why?' She lowered her voice. 'Has she found out?'

'I don't know what you mean,' I said sternly. 'But if you don't stop I shall have to remove your name from my list.'

'You'd still be in my dreams,' she said, 'and I'd see you driving about.'

'That may be. But you're not to write any more letters. Now, what have you come to consult me about?'

'Oh! nothing. I thought you'd like to see me.'

'Miss Trotter,' I said, standing up. 'I'm extremely busy. Please don't come here wasting my time for nothing.'

'Then it's all over between us.'

'Don't be ridiculous. Good-morning.'

'I never thought it would end like this.'

I opened the door for her and as she passed she gave me a reproachful look. 'I reely never did.'

I made a note to remove her name from my list before she started making wild accusations about me, and I got hauled before the Executive Council.

I had seen about fifteen patients when a young woman in drainpipe trousers and sunglasses, with a scarf tied tightly round her head, came in.

As soon as she had sat down facing me on the chair, she took off the glasses, which had been practically obscuring her face, and removed the headscarf. Her blonde hair fell to her shoulders.

'Tessa!' I said. 'Tessa Brindley. What are you doing here?'

What I really meant was, 'What are you doing here all dressed up like that?' She was, after all, my patient and had a perfect right to consult me.

She smiled. 'Oh! the disguise,' she said. 'I didn't particularly want anyone to see me coming here in case it got back to Daddy.'

'What happened to you last night? Your father phoned me. He was worried because you didn't go straight home.'

'Yes. I'm sorry about that. It's all rather a long story, but I'll tell you, then you'll understand about last night. I owe your wife an apology. It was very rude of me to leave like that.'

I watched her. She looked as if she had been crying, but it did nothing to impair her beauty; only made it sadder.

'I'm at your disposal.'

She looked at the cherry-red headscarf and the black glasses on her lap, then straight at me.

'I'm going to have a baby,' she said.

Sitting there, wrapped in my professional composure which allowed me to show neither surprise nor dismay, I felt chiefly pity for H H Brindley, who would have to face a fallen idol.

'Are you sure, Tessa?'

'It's three months now. Nobody knows, of course, except me and...'

'The father?'

She nodded.

'Do your parents know anything about him?'

'About Tony? No. Daddy wouldn't approve of Tony,' she said bitterly. 'He's not wealthy; he's quiet, serious; what Daddy would call "very ordinerry." He's a journalist.'

'You know, Tessa,' I said, 'I think you've got your father wrong. He loves you very much and you're his only daughter. He'd give anything to see you happily married to the right man. I'm quite sure that the fact that he had no money wouldn't matter at all.'

Looking at her, I couldn't fit her into the picture HH had painted for me of Tessa, rocking and rolling and spending hours in coffee bars with long-haired youths. I told her how worried he had been about the company she kept.

'Oh! that.' She laughed. 'That was just my alibi for spending the time with Tony. It was the sort of story he could never check up on. I hate rock and roll.'

'But you love Tony?'

'Yes,' she said, 'I love Tony.'

'Well,' I said, 'there seems nothing for it but for you to take Tony home and tell your father everything and that you want to get married. I'm sure he loves you enough to get over the shock about the baby.'

Tessa looked at me. 'I'm afraid it isn't as simple as that,' she said. 'You see, Tony's already married.'

For a moment I could think of nothing to say. The poor girl had certainly landed herself with a lot of trouble.

'Please don't worry about Daddy,' she said. 'I know I shall have to settle that problem myself. I came to ask you what to do about the baby.'

'You mean...'

She was shaking her head. 'No, I don't. I

just want to know where I can have it. Somewhere quiet, not too public.'

Tessa was a very brave girl. I examined her to confirm about the baby, and found it was all just as she had said.

'What has Tony got to say about it?' I asked her.

'I only told him last night. I went to meet him after I left here. We sat in the car arguing until half past two. He doesn't love his wife, but he has two young children at school. It wasn't that I thought he would ever marry me. I knew all the time that it wasn't possible. But I thought he ought to know about the baby, and when he did he wanted me to get rid of it. He said he could raise enough money for that, and I needn't even tell Daddy. He couldn't understand why I couldn't agree. I think,' she said, 'perhaps he doesn't love me as much as I love him.'

'Look, Tessa,' I said, 'about having the baby. I think it would be a good idea to wait until you've told your parents before we make any arrangements.' What I really meant was that if H H Brindley was going to do anything as stupid as to cut her off with a shilling, the arrangements were going to be very different from those we could fix up if he were willing to stand by her financially. I wanted to be sure, too, that she did confide in him quickly. It wasn't a nice situation to cope with alone, especially at eighteen.

'Just as you think,' Tessa said, standing up, 'and thank you for your help. I know that this is all my fault and I can't expect anyone to wave a magic wand and get me out of this mess. I did want to be sure that everything would be all right about the baby, though.' She put on her dark glasses and said shyly, 'I don't know much about babies.'

When she had put on her headscarf again and had gone, I thought what a pity it was that in cases like Tessa's I couldn't wave a magic wand. It was clear from where she had inherited her courage and singleness of purpose. It seemed sad that a girl like Tessa Brindley, who held every winning card in the pack, should have started out on the wrong foot. She must have been very much in love with Tony.

I was on rota for the three women practitioners in the district. One of the messages Sylvia had taken was for me to see a patient of Doctor Phœbe Miller's. He was an old man complaining of a sore chest.

The house was a very large, old-fashioned, rambling one in a street of such houses owned by the more wealthy inhabitants of the district. Most of them were freshly painted and had well-tended drives in which stood large, glossy car Number One, if the master was at home, or small, easy-to-park car Number Two waiting to take madam shopping. Sometimes, like mother and child, both waited patiently before the front door. Number sixteen, belonging to Mr Pompey Lodwick, stood out from the rest, chiefly because the house looked neglected, the drive sprouted tufts of grass, and there was neither Number One nor Number Two car to be seen.

I was surprised when the door was opened by a young and exceedingly brassy blonde, who looked as if she had escaped from the second row of the chorus; she was smoking a cigarette in a jewelled holder and seemed surprised to see me.

'Yes?' she said.

'I'm the doctor.'

She patted her hair, licked her lips, threw out her not inconsiderable bosom and smiled. 'I was expectin' the lady,' she said.

'Doctor Miller's off duty today; I'm doing her work,' I explained. 'I've come to see Mr Lodwick.'

'Come in,' she said; 'I'll call the old sod.'

She showed me into a large room in which the curtains were drawn, letting in only a glimmer of daylight; the furniture was shrouded with dust covers and everything smelled musty.

'Sorry about this,' she said, 'but the mean old buzzard doesn't want his carpet to fade or anyone to sit on his chairs.' She shuddered. 'I sometimes wonder why I stick it.'

She left me alone, and I wandered round

peering at dusty Dresden shepherdesses and old copies of old magazines. It was very depressing. In the bay window was a grand piano also wearing a shroud. I lifted the lid of the keyboard and played chopsticks on the stiff, yellowed keys. I didn't hear the old man come in, but when I looked round he was standing beside me in the grubbiest dressing-gown I had ever seen. I closed the piano carefully and, I hoped, nonchalantly, and introduced myself to Mr Pompey Lodwick.

'I understand it's your chest,' I said, taking out my stethoscope. 'Shall we have a look at you?' I indicated the shrouded sofa for him to lie on and went over to draw the curtains so that I could see what I was doing.

'No!' the old man shouted. 'My carpet!'

'Very well,' I said, 'I'll put the light on.'

'Are you mad? It's broad daylight outside. Don't you know that electricity costs money?'

'Well, it's one or the other,' I said, getting fed up, and pulled back the curtain, nearly choking from the dust.

There was very little wrong with the old man's chest, but I said I would give him some linctus to soothe the soreness, and began to write a prescription.

'You're wasting your time,' Blondie said from where she was leaning seductively against the door watching me. 'He won't get it, whatever it is you're giving him.'

'Why?'

'The shilling.'

'That's his lookout,' I said, anxious to escape from the spine-chilling atmosphere, and thrust the prescription into his hand. 'Take two teaspoonfuls three times a day,' I said and, having done my duty, put away my pen. Pompey Lodwick wasn't listening but was carefully rolling my prescription into a narrow spill.

'For the gas,' Blondie explained.

Mr Lodwick shuffled over to the mantelpiece in his threadbare carpet slippers and laid the spill down carefully. He looked at Blondie. 'Perhaps you wouldn't mind going upstairs for my spectacles,' he said. She winked at me and left the room.

'I'll be going, too,' I said, fastening my case.

'Oh! no.' He gripped my arm and, looking over his shoulder to make sure that Blondie had gone, took something from his dressing-gown pocket.

'Look,' he said, 'here's something that will interest you.'

I looked, and he flicked through a most amazing collection of pornographic pictures, chuckling as he did so.

I made for the door. Outside, Blondie was waiting with the glasses, the sides of which were bound with sticking plaster.

She opened her mouth to say something,

but the old man called out:

'Jessie! You come in here! The doctor can see himself out. You're never so anxious when it's Doctor Phœbe.'

She shrugged her shoulders resignedly and blew me a kiss.

Late that night I rang Doctor Miller to tell her about the patients I had seen for her.

'That was a nasty old man you sent me to see,' I said; 'Mr Lodwick.'

She laughed. 'Sorry about that. Has he still got the little blonde girl with him?'

'Yes, why?'

'Just wondered. He changes them every time he changes his underwear, which isn't very often. He has a greatly increased libido because of an enlarged prostate. Fortunately his bark is worse than his bite.' Phœbe guffawed in her hearty manner. 'As a matter of fact, he hasn't any bite at all, poor man. The last but one, a little ginger lady, told me.'

'Is he really as hard up as he makes out?'

This time Phœbe's laugh nearly burst my eardrums. I held the receiver away until she had calmed down.

'Pompey Lodwick,' she said, 'poor? My dear young man, he practically owns the entire district.'

'Well,' I said, 'I hope he doesn't get ill again on your day off.'

Thirteen

A few days later I was more than surprised to receive a letter from a firm of solicitors called Curly, Curly & Bright. Messrs Curly, Curly & Bright had been instructed to write to me by their client, Mr Pompey Lodwick, whose house, they said, I had visited in my professional capacity on the 15th inst. Even the thought of the mean old Mr Lodwick in his sunless old house made me remember my visit to him with the greatest distaste. What Messrs Curly, Curly & Bright had to say caused me to regard it with positive loathing. I could hardly believe that the letter was not intended as a joke, but then I remembered Mr Lodwick. I doubted if he had regarded my visit to his miserable old house as anything but funny. He was probably trying to get his own back for the unspeakable things he imagined I had done during my three and a half seconds alone with Blondie.

Our client informs us, *wrote Messrs Curly, Curly & Bright* that during your visit to his house on the above date you assaulted his rosewood piano (Bechstein Grand) with the result that the instrument sustained considerable damage.

The cost of repairing the said piano is Two pounds Ten Shillings and Sixpence and our client looks to you for payment of that amount.

We shall be glad to receive your cheque for this sum, failing which would you kindly give us the name of your solicitor who will accept service of proceedings.

Yours faithfully,

ISOBEL JONES,

p.p. Florian Curly
of Messrs Curly, Curly & Bright.

I made up my mind never again to play chopsticks uninvited, and since I was sure that nobody would ever invite me, blamed Mr Pompey Lodwick for bringing my musical aspirations to an untimely end.

I rang Phœbe Miller, since the old man was her patient, and told her what had happened, and also, jokingly, that she was liable for the two pounds ten and six since she was technically responsible for my actions in the capacity of her locum. Never at a loss, she replied promptly that if I persisted in going round assaulting pianos she would have to suggest to the others that my name be removed from the rota. She then laughed heartily and said not to worry; she would deal with Mr Lodwick and she could guarantee I would hear no more from Curly, Curly & Bright.

'How can you be so sure?' I asked, curious.

'Ways and means,' she said mysteriously. 'When you've been in practice as long as I have you'll have them eating out of your hand too. Even the grubby, libidinous old Pompey Lodwicks.'

I still don't know what she threatened him with, but I never heard any more of either Pompey Lodwick or his decrepit piano. The incident left its mark, however, and since then I have confined my curiosity over other people's possessions to the visual. Many is the time I have stood alone in various lounges, halls or dining-rooms and clasped my itching hands firmly behind my back before a vase I could swear was Ming, or a Picasso print which I was convinced was hung the wrong way up. I even stopped, for a while, perching my thirteen and a half stone on occasional tables while I wrote prescriptions, and for the first time was careful where I put my case. I had no desire to be branded as an 'assaulter' of my patients' belongings, and the name of Pompey Lodwick lingered for quite a while in my mind.

I was getting into the car, ready to do the morning visits, when I heard the familiar eight-cylinder, throaty boom-boom-boom of Archibald Compton's Allard coming down the road. Deciding to ignore the now familiar, condescending wave of yellow string glove as we passed each other on our rounds, I busied myself with some Elastoplast tins on the back seat. To my surprise, the Allard pulled up behind me and Compton, all hair-cream and smiles, stuck his head through my opened window.

'Morning,' he said affably; 'I was going to ring you.'

'Oh! yes?' I looked to see if there was any Elastoplast in a tin which I could feel was empty.

'A little girl came to see me. Wants to transfer to my list. Said she knew you wouldn't mind.'

'Who's that?' I said, trying to think of any small girls I might have offended lately.

'A Miss Trotter.'

'Oh! her!' I said ungrammatically. I might have known he'd been referring to a big little girl.

'Yes. I wouldn't have mentioned it except that she's got a lump in the breast. I've had her admitted and Scriven's doing a biopsy this afternoon.'

'A lump in the breast!' He now had my attention. 'I don't think I've ever examined her,' I said. 'She's never complained of anything.'

Archibald Compton examined his gloves carefully.

'That's odd,' he said; 'she told me she'd

not only been to see you in the surgery but that you'd been in "constant touch."'

He waited for an explanation.

'She's nutty,' I said, pulling out the starter; 'she thinks she's in love with me.'

'Oh!' Compton said. 'How strange. She told me she couldn't stand the sight of you.'

I shrugged and pulled the starter again, nothing having happened the first time. 'I must rush,' I said against the agonised throbbing of my engine. 'I'm sorry about Renee Trotter, but as a patient you're welcome to her.'

He stood watching me as I drove off. He looked sad. Whether he was grieving for my medical incompetence or the fact that I imagined all my young girl patients to be in love with me, I don't know. With my mind on Renee Trotter, I had again forgotten to ask him about the Hart family. After a meeting with Doctor Compton I always felt prickly and irritated. Whether it was his superior air or his calm assurance of making good in the district, I don't know, but in any of our brief encounters I always seemed to lose on points.

I did my visits with frequent glances at various clocks on various walls and mantelpieces, and with half my mind on Sylvia. She had been worrying me a little lately as she had been getting frequent headaches which she said were quite unpleasant, and in view of her raised blood pressure I wasn't too happy about her. She laughed at me for chasing her round with my sphygmomanometer at frequent intervals. I didn't let her see, as I took her blood pressure, that I didn't consider it a laughing matter. This morning I had sent her off for an extra visit to Mr Humphrey Mallow and was waiting for twelve o'clock, when she should be back, to see what he had to say about her.

I went home between an asthma injection and a whooping baby and found Sylvia in the bedroom, packing a small case.

'Oh! Sweetie,' she said, coming to put her arms round my neck although we couldn't get as close to each other as before, 'I've got to go into hospital for some investigations. They've got a bed this afternoon. You've to phone Humphrey and he'll tell you what it's all about.'

Upset, I rang Mr Mallow immediately. He told me that because of her high blood pressure and headaches he wanted to take her into hospital for a couple of days to make sure that she had no kidney trouble. He was certainly taking every care.

'What is it?' Sylvia said when I'd put the phone down. 'Will I be all right?'

'Of course you will. It's just that it's more comfortable to have these tests while you're lying in bed in the hospital than to hang around the draughty corridors as an outpatient.'

'What about the baby?'

'What about it?'

'There won't be any trouble, will there?'

'None at all,' I said, more light-heartedly than I felt. 'By this time next year we'll be deafened by the patter of tiny feet.'

Sylvia smiled.

'What are you laughing at?' I said.

'You. They don't patter at seven months.'

'Ours will.'

They had no private room available at the hospital, and since Humphrey Mallow wanted the tests done immediately, Sylvia had agreed to go into the ward for a couple of days. I left her by her bed between a large grey-haired woman who was sitting up knitting and a pale-faced girl who watched from her pillow with sad dark eyes, and went outside while she got into bed.

When the mousey-haired probationer told me she was ready, I went back and found her sitting in bed, demure in a pink and white striped nightdress.

'Don't look so sad,' she said, taking my hand as I sat on the bed. The woman next door knitted extra busily, pretending not to listen.

'I'm not. It's just that I'm not used to seeing you in that hospital nightie.'

Sylvia laughed. I couldn't see the joke.

'You are a pet,' she said. 'It's not a hospital one. I bought it specially on my way home this morning. I didn't seem to have anything in my trousseau suitable for sitting up in a general ward. So you needn't feel the slightest bit sorry for me.'

I was just about to say something when the knitting woman, without interrupting the rhythm of her needles, said:

'She'll be all right, dear. We all look after each other here.'

She jerked her head towards the young woman on the other side of Sylvia. 'She only got done this morning. She's not prop'ly round yet. I'll give 'er a drop of my Lucozade later.'

The rest of the day passed slowly. As I finished my work I felt worried and upset as I thought of Sylvia in the hospital. For the first time I knew what it felt like to be a patient when one of the family was ill, and I didn't like it a bit. I thought of the number of people I shunted daily off to hospitals, and the number of relatives I told glibly how happy and well looked after they'd be. Next time I wouldn't be quite so glib.

I ate my dinner in a quiet house, lonely at the dining-room table. With Sylvia away, even Iris seemed to have lost some of her bounce and came despondently in and out with the dishes. While I was eating my dessert which came out of a tin she had opened, there was a ring at the front door. Iris said it was a Mr Brindley who wanted to see me urgently.

Worried about Sylvia, I felt I wasn't in the mood for H H Brindley's problems, but told Iris to put him in the drawing-room. When I joined him his appearance gave me a shock and my concern for Sylvia slid temporarily into the background.

Sartorially he looked the same, from his highly polished, handmade shoes to his perfectly folded breast-pocket handkerchief with its maroon HH neatly embroidered. Inside his clothes he stood like an old man. His voice had lost its bombast. He came straight to the point.

'You know about our Tessa.' It wasn't a question.

I pulled up a chair for him and switched on the stove.

'Yes,' I said.

It seemed to have hit him even harder than I had thought it would.

'She told you the name of the father?'

'Yes,' I said, without realising the implications of his question.

'Well, you'd better tell it to me. I can't get nowt out of Tessa.'

'I only know his Christian name,' I said, now understanding what he was getting at.

'That'll do,' he said. 'It's a start, any road. It won't take H H Brindley long to find him.'

'Look,' I said, 'what good will it do?'

'It won't do him much good.' Brindley's

eyes were sharp with anger. 'I'll break every bone in his body.'

'I'm sorry,' I said, 'but I can't tell you his name if Tessa doesn't want you to know.'

'Tommyrot,' he said, getting angry. 'Tessa's a child. I don't care what she's done, she's still a child, and she doesn't know what she's talking about.'

'That may be,' I said, 'but what Tessa told me was in confidence and I'm bound by the tradition of professional secrecy.'

'Professional–!' he said. 'Whether you tell me or not I'll find him. It'll just take me a bit longer with nothing to work on. I'll find him if it's the last thing I do on this earth.'

'Well, I'm sorry,' I said, 'but there's no question of me telling you his name. If Tessa doesn't want you to know, there's nothing I can do to help.'

He said, more quietly: 'Tessa says if I try to find out who it is she'll kill herself. You don't think she's serious, do you?'

'She may very well be,' I said. 'She's emotionally perturbed. She's worried; anxious about the future...'

He held up his hand. 'Don't you think I know?' he said slowly, 'I'd have given anything, anything at all, to see my girl happily married. That's why I'm so dead set on finding the chap that's done this to her.'

'But if it's going to make Tessa even more unhappy?' I said.

'Tessa won't know,' he said determinedly. 'But me mind's made up: I've only the one daughter and I'm going to find this chap. He's a married man and he should of known better. Tessa should have known better too, but that's neither here nor there. Tessa's suffering for it, and if H H Brindley tells you this young man, and I don't care who he is, isn't going to get off scot- free, he means it.'

'What are we going to do about Tessa?' I said, in an effort to calm him down.

'Whatever you say. You're her doctor, and she wants no one but you to look after her.'

'Don't you want her to see an obstetrician?' I asked, knowing that people like the Brindleys usually wanted specialised attention.

'Tessa says she wants no one but you. You do deliver babies, don't you?'

'Yes, I do. I could take her into a private nursing home or she could have it at home. In the circumstances...'

'I shall be sending her down to our country place,' Brindley said; 'it only takes an hour by car from here. I want you to look after her for me.'

I hesitated. In his customary manner, a result of his own life story, he misinterpreted my silence.

'I don't care what it costs.'

'It isn't that,' I said. 'It's just the journey. If I happen to be busy...'

'Please don't refuse,' he said, sufficiently worried to be asking instead of demanding. 'I know it's not very convenient. But Tessa seems to be pinning her hopes on you. She said you'd stand by her. There's a nursing home nearby,' he said hopefully.

'All right,' I said, unable to refuse. 'What's going to happen when she's had the baby?'

H H Brindley stood up. 'We shall see when the time comes, if not before,' he said, and by the threat in his voice I knew that he was determined to find Tony. 'My main concern is Tessa.' He looked at me with a plea for reassurance in his eyes. 'She'll be all right, won't she? Our little Tessa.'

'I see no reason why she shouldn't be.'

'You'll come whenever she needs you then?'

'Yes,' I said, 'don't worry.'

'No matter what?'

'No matter what,' I promised.

'That's one thing off me mind then. Tessa'll be glad.'

At the door he said: 'Sorry for taking up your leisure time.'

'Only too pleased to help,' I said.

He put his hands in his pockets and stepped on to the path.

'It's tekken the wind out o' me sails, rather.'

I felt pity for him as I watched him go.

Fourteen

Without Sylvia the house felt horrible, and I couldn't imagine how I had managed on my own for a year while waiting for her to say 'Yes.' I was cold in bed, had no one to talk to, and noticed that Iris put the milk on the table in the bottle and wandered round the house in her slippers. Yet it was more than just that. On the second day I had a hot-water bottle, told Iris she looked sloppy and had Loveday round to keep me company, but it was no better. It was obvious that what I was missing was what was commonly known as my 'better half,' and that no calculated accumulation of the comforts she provided could compensate for her flesh-and-blood presence. I discussed with Loveday the peculiarities of marriage.

'It's odd,' I said, 'how one particular woman, for no one particular reason, is the right one.'

Loveday, always loyal, didn't think it at all odd.

'It's purely a question of genes,' he said, examining the glowing end of his cigar, 'or instinct, if you like. Marriage is rarely a rational process. A man thinks he loves a woman for her hair, her glorious eyes, and concord of their thoughts; a woman thinks she loves a man because of his self-confidence, his helplessness or his child-like solemnities, but what has really happened has been that in some mysterious way beyond our ken, 3,000 genes which constitute the blueprint of him have conferred with her 3,200 in secret sessions of intense emotion, and have come to the conclusion that if each sends about 1,500 of their number they may, with luck, produce something which will stagger on with the race.'

'So for "love" substitute the mutual attraction of the genes?'

Loveday nodded.

'That's right. Otherwise, how on earth could you account for the hundreds of most presentable men who choose the oddest-looking wives or the good-looking women who settle for ugly, roly-poly men?' He sat forward in his chair. 'If I were to provide you with an identical, physical copy of Sylvia now, but one composed of a different set of genes, do you think she'd be acceptable?'

'Of course not.'

'Well, there you are,' he said, and held out his glass. 'What about some more of that apricot brandy?'

I poured out his brandy and thought of what he had said. He was probably right in his theory about the genes, but I had been married too recently to want to reduce marriage to such logical terms. It made me remember a party, given by one of Sylvia's model friends, to which we had gone shortly before our marriage. The friend had met us at the door and warned us that she wanted the party to be exceptionally gay, and that we must separate for the evening. Sylvia and I, willing to enter into the spirit of the thing, had kissed each other goodbye in the hallway and agreed that it was our last chance to see if we could find anyone we liked better. It was a large party and, as parties go, had everything. I danced with some of the most beautiful girls in London who were more than willing to twine their arms round my neck and lead me into corners; had a session at the bar to see if perhaps my soberness accounted for my distinct reluctance to be led into corners; and ended the evening sitting on the floor discussing Existentialism with a wide-eyed brunette who was both pretty and intelligent. I laughed, drank, ate sausages on sticks and did the cha-cha, trying not to look too often to see what Sylvia was doing. I did my genuine best to imagine I was fancy-free and having the most wonderful time, yet the only highlights of the evening were when I allowed myself a quick glance in Sylvia's direction and invariably found her eyes searching for mine. When the evening was over we thanked our hostess politely and with as much enthusiasm as we could manage and escaped into the darkness of the early morning. Driving home, we sat close together in silence, each a little stunned to have discovered how useless we were without each other.

'Well,' I said to Loveday, 'you can stick to your genes; I still prefer to call it love.'

'It doesn't matter two hoots what you call it. It comes to the same thing.'

A thought occurred to me. 'And when marriages go on the rocks,' I said, 'which started off knee-deep in love?'

'The attraction of the genes,' Loveday said, 'is only a start. It's the thing that makes Mr Jones' habit of going to bed in his socks bearable to Mrs Jones in the first years of marriage. Under the powerful mutual attractions they have for each other she probably doesn't even notice.'

'And after the first years?'

'Then this thing that you, with stars still in your eyes, call love at first sight, and I put down to chemical reaction, begins to wear off and one of two things will happen. If Mrs Jones has any sense she will realise that, although Mr Jones goes to bed in his socks, which she hates, he is still the same Tom, Dick or Harry she agreed to marry and that he still enjoys her company, works cheerfully to keep her and helps her with the washing-up. She'll put up with the socks, tell him frequently what a good sort he is, and discover suddenly that the more she tells him the better he is, and they'll have every chance of living really happily ever after. If Mrs Jones hasn't any sense – if she refuses to grow up with the years and wants to remain the self-centred girl she was, she'll close her eyes to his good points, nag him about his horrible habits and will suddenly wake up one day to the fact that he doesn't even help her with the washing-up any more but toddles down to the pub. Then all you have left is the stuff of which unfortunately most marriages seem to consist: Mr and Mrs Jones, two strangers, sharing nothing but a name, jogging along in various stages of animosity from the benign to the malevolent, under the same roof.'

'Aren't you being a little cynical?' I said. 'After all, I can't see why just because Mr Jones goes to bed in his socks the marriage has to break up.'

'But then you aren't Mrs Jones,' Loveday said, 'and anyway the socks are only the jumping-off point. If you think they are the slightest bit unimportant go and sit for a day in the divorce courts. If it isn't Mr Jones' socks, it is Mrs Jones' natural verbosity which her husband once thought so attractive, that provides the first spark.' Loveday carefully broke the long ash from his cigar into an ashtray.

'Nothing continues to grow without a little encouragement,' he said seriously, 'not even love. It just dries up.'

I smiled.

'It's no laughing matter,' Loveday said. 'Marriage may be a funny institution but it has to be taken seriously. If it's to work, that is.'

I was just about to pursue the conversation further when the phone, which was at Loveday's elbow, rang. He picked up the receiver.

'No, I'm not the doctor,' he said, then 'Thank God' to me and handed me the phone.

It was the district midwife phoning from the home of a patient whose baby I had promised to deliver.

Loveday followed me into the surgery and watched while I checked my equipment: rubber gloves, forceps...

'Big stuff,' Loveday said.

'It won't be necessary. She's a hefty multip. This is her sixth, I think – sixth or seventh, I always lose count.'

'Good Lord!' Loveday said. 'I didn't think that sort of thing happened nowadays.'

'She's an Italian girl. Married an English chap who was over there in the army. It doesn't seem to worry her. She's crazy about all those children but homesick for Italy. The neighbours leave her alone rather: our usual attitude to foreigners. They think there's something a bit odd about her when she goes on producing a child year after year, and give her a wide berth.'

'Ha!' Loveday said.

'Unintentional,' I said. 'Make yourself comfortable; I don't suppose I shall be long. The child will most probably have fallen out by the time I get there; she's second-staging already.'

'I'll wait a bit. If you're too long you may have to buy yourself another bottle of apricot brandy.'

He saw me off at the front door, and shivered in the night air.

'Thank God I decided on dentistry,' he said. 'Nine till five, five days a week.'

'Don't pity me,' I called from the car. 'I like it.'

And it was true. At home, sitting before the fire with Loveday, I had felt sleepy, lethargic, looking forward to nothing so much as bed. Now I was awake, exhilarated almost, because I was working and I liked my job.

The single street lamp threw eerie shadows down the tiny cul-de-sac on the Council estate.

The door of number twelve was open. On the stairs, in underwear and a variety of odd jumpers which represented their night attire, sat four of Graziella Smith's five or six children.

‘’Allo, Doc!’ said the eldest, who went to school.

A small one said: ‘Ciaou!’ shyly and buried her face in her sister’s lap.

Upstairs Graziella was rolling her mountainous frame in the bed and moaning: ‘Mamma mia, Mamma mia, Mamma mia!’

‘Push, dear!’ Sister Mildmay was saying calmly from the end of the bed.

‘Mamma mia, Mamma mia, Mamma mia!’ Graziella acknowledged me with her eyes but was too busy to say anything.

I took off my jacket, rolled up my sleeves and went into the bathroom to get scrubbed up. When I came back Graziella, with the help of Sister Mildmay, had given birth to a large boy baby.

‘Too late!’ Sister Mildmay said triumphantly.

‘Don’t swank,’ I said. ‘You didn’t give me much of a chance.’

‘I only just got here myself,’ she said, working competently. ‘She’s been having pains all day but didn’t say anything.’

While Sister Mildmay dealt with the baby who was now screwing up his ugly little face and crying, I waited for the expulsion of the afterbirth. I doubted if Loveday would have made much headway with the apricot brandy before I was back with him.

‘Where’s Mr Smith?’ I asked.

Sister Mildmay said something, but just

then the woman in the house next door started to shout at her husband and a stream of swear words came clearly through the thin dividing wall.

When it was quiet again, except for the tiny wail of the baby, Sister told me that a neighbour had gone to fetch Graziella's husband from his work where he was on night shift.

Ten minutes later, Sister Mildmay, still making soothing noises, was setting the baby in its basket on the floor.

'She seems to be bleeding fairly heavily,' I said. 'Will you check her blood pressure for me, Sister, if the baby's all right?'

It began to look as if everything wasn't to be quite as straightforward as I had imagined. As the bleeding increased, I examined the abdomen and found that the afterbirth was incompletely separated from the uterus.

'I'm going to try to expel it,' I said.

Sister Mildmay wound the cuff of the sphygmomanometer skilfully round Graziella's arm. The baby stopped crying and it was suddenly quiet.

'BP's falling,' Sister Mildmay said, 'and she's looking awfully pale.'

I straightened up, having been unsuccessful in my attempt to remove the placenta.

'She's lost roughly two pints, I should say.' Sister Mildmay bustled round trying to reduce the chaos but keeping one eye on the patient.

The baby, the basket in the corner tilted so that its feet were raised above its head, started to cry again, then stopped. Outside one of the children began to whimper, 'Mamma! Mamma!'

'See if you can get them into bed,' I said. 'We shall probably be here for some time.'

When Sister Mildmay came back it was obvious that I was going to need some help in removing the placenta because it would have to be done with an anæsthetic. The bleeding hadn't stopped and Graziella would also need a blood transfusion. I went out to the call-box to ring the Obstetric Flying Squad. This service was an extremely useful one to general practitioners who did midwifery. It consisted of an ambulance which was always at the ready, an obstetric house surgeon, supplies of blood for transfusions, and extra nurses. For Graziella Smith I needed the help of the obstetrician so that one of us could give the anæsthetic while the other manually removed the placenta, and some blood to replace that which she had lost.

Back in the bedroom we waited. Graziella was almost unconscious. She had lost about four pints of blood and her pulse was barely palpable. I strained my ears for the sound of the ambulance bell and thought I heard it;

the woman next door began to swear again and I wasn't sure. I went down to the front door to look.

The white ambulance, ghostly in the lamplight, turned into the cul-de-sac. Its doors opened and down the steps ran three dark-cloaked nurses each carrying part of the equipment necessary for the blood transfusion. Following them, also hurrying, came the white-coated doctor.

'Hovis Brown!' I exclaimed as he passed under the street lamp.

He looked at me but didn't slow down.

'Good Lord!' he said. 'It's you!'

We had no time for further conversation except about our patient.

Hovis and his organisation somehow managed not to fall over each other in the tiny bedroom, and we set about our first job of replacing some of the blood which Graziella had lost and was still losing.

With some trepidation, I tried to get the transfusion needle, through which the blood would flow, into the vein in Graziella's arm. Her blood pressure was by now so low that the vein was practically collapsed. To my surprise I managed it at the first attempt and released the clip on the tube which connected the needle with the bottle of blood. It began to flow rapidly.

When the first bottle of blood was empty we replaced it with a second, a third and then a fourth. While it was flowing we got everything ready for the removal of the placenta.

By the time she had received the contents of the fourth bottle of blood Graziella's blood pressure had risen and her pulse was strong enough for what we had to do.

I administered the chloroform on an open mask while Hovis, masked and gowned, removed the placenta from the birth canal.

I gave her an injection. Almost immediately the womb contracted and the bleeding, which had now been going on for over an hour, stopped.

Graziella who, because of the loss of blood, had been unaware of what had been happening, heaved herself up.

'Cosa c'é?' she said. Then looked round at all of us. 'Watta matta, Dottore?'

'Nothing at all,' I said. 'You just lost a little blood which we had to replace.' I pointed to the corner. 'You have a lovely little boy.'

She looked suspiciously at Hovis' white gown. 'I seeck, me?'

'Not at all. You're fine. Bella!'

'Grazie,' she said and sank back. 'Multa stanca...'

It was hardly surprising that she was tired.

The crisis over, Hovis and I went down to the kitchen, leaving the nurses to tidy up Graziella, and the chaos. One of his organisation had made coffee and was raiding Graziella's larder for the sugar which she couldn't find.

'That's some set-up you've got,' I said to Hovis whom I hadn't seen since our student days, and whose real name I was unable to remember. 'I've never had to use it before.'

'Always ready to oblige,' he said, his hair as blond as ever, if thinner, and sticking out at right angles from his florid face.

'I must say I was pleased to see you.'

He sipped his coffee. 'Ugh!' he said. 'You let the milk boil, Nurse. Everybody always is.'

'Her pulse was nearly non-existent,' I said, still surprised at the hæmorrhage Graziella had decided to have.

'Don't let it worry you,' Hovis said; 'just send for Uncle Hovis and his concert party.'

His facetiousness reminded me of Faraday.

'You hospital doctors are all the same,' I said; 'you never see a patient more than once or twice. It's all the same to you if they live or die!'

'By that I gather you're wearing yourself out in GP,' Hovis said.

I nodded. 'At least I know the names of my patients. It's not just 'that woman up in Florence Nightingale with the carcinoma of the pancreas or the old boy in William Pitt with the pulmonary embolism.'

'I never could remember names, anyway,' Hovis said, 'so it's just as well I'm not in your line.'

The nurse refilled our coffee cups, then

Hovis said: 'By the way, have you any idea what happened to Spiky O'Flanagan?'

I remembered the tufty-haired Irishman who had been in our year and who had been more preoccupied than most of us with the pursuit of skirts.

'Didn't he marry that girl he got into trouble, and buy a practice in Melbourne?'

'Maybe. What do you think of Marshlake getting a consultantship at the National?'

We finished the coffee before we had exhausted the long list of acquaintances with whom we had sweated away the long years in hospital and sworn never to lose touch with but, after qualifying, had never seen again.

As we stood up, stretching, to go and have another look at the patient, Hovis said: 'By the way, haven't you got a fellow called Archie Compton somewhere round here?'

I felt my hackles rise. 'Yes. Do you know him?'

'We were together while I was doing my fellowship. He was with Sir Peter Tollings for a couple of years – the apple of his eye.'

'So he does know something about skins, then?'

'I should say. As much as Sir Peter, if not more. Felt he had to have a change, though, after the accident. Went to pieces, poor fellow. I heard he was having a shot at GP round here.'

'What accident?' We stood in the tiny

hallway where the red wallpaper was peeling at child level.

'Didn't you know? His wife and baby were both killed in that train smash at Wapping. Nice girl. Pretty. He brought her up to the hospital once or twice before they were married. Hart, I think her name was. Pamela or Muriel or something. Terribly, terribly sad!'

'Hart?'

'Think so. Let's see what's going on upstairs.'

The room was now magically tidy and the patient, in a neatly made bed, was sleeping soundly.

The hospital nurses put on their capes and gathered up the equipment they had brought. Together, with Hovis, they disappeared as efficiently as they had come, if less urgently.

'Well,' Sister Mildmay said, 'we didn't expect that.' She leaned over to look at the baby. 'Bonny little chap!'

I left her to wait for Mr Smith and set off in the quiet night for home, my brain whirling with thoughts of Graziella Smith's *post partum* hæmorrhage, Hovis Brown, Sylvia, and Archibald Compton. I passed the traffic lights at red; fortunately the road was deserted.

When I got home Loveday had gone; so had half the apricot brandy.

Fifteen

It was good to have Sylvia home. The house felt normal again and I was able to relax.

The busy flow of flus, coughs and colds was beginning, with the warmer weather, to die down and I was usually able to finish most of my visits in the mornings. In my free afternoon hours I decided, since time was getting on, to paint the small, sunny room we had agreed to make into the nursery. There had been no difficulty in selecting which room the new addition was to occupy; the trouble started when I had to decide upon the paint. Not that it was really trouble, but a sort of clashing undercurrent of wills that never quite came out into the open.

It had begun with what Humphrey Mallow had told us when Sylvia came out of the hospital.

The tests he had carried out showed that she had no kidney lesion, but in view of the hypertension and the headaches she was getting because of it, he had told us both that he would strongly advise us, in Sylvia's interest, to content ourselves with one child. We were both a little disappointed as we had always visualised ourselves with a large family, at any rate anything up to four. It wasn't long, though, before we both managed to reorientate our ideas and came to the conclusion that if we produced one healthy baby and Sylvia remained well we should both be very happy. One evening, though, we discovered quite by chance that we each had very different ideas about what was to be our only child.

I had had a particularly long and arduous surgery during the course of which I had seen an acute appendix and an early pneumonia, both of which had held me up. It was nearly nine o'clock, and I had been going on steadily since six, when I pressed the buzzer for the last patient. It was not a patient: it was a young man with an enormous handlebar moustache and a briefcase, who travelled for one of the drug houses. He bounced in jauntily, although he must have been waiting patiently to see me for over an hour.

'No, Mr Piper,' I said wearily, totting up in the day book the number of patients I had seen. 'Not tonight. I'm too tired and I'd like to have my dinner. Call in later in the week, there's a good chap.'

Mr Piper, sitting on the examination couch, was already unfastening the straps of his briefcase. He was one of the more persistent of the drug firm representatives, who phoned, called or waited patiently until one's resistance was so worn down that it was usually quicker to let them have their say than argue.

That night, though, I was determined. Since Mr Piper had developed, by virtue of his calling, a hide like a rhinoceros and was completely impervious to hints, I stood up and held open the door firmly.

With the speed and sleight of hand of a conjuror, he had strewn the couch with an assortment of highly coloured literature.

'I won't keep you one moment, Doctor,' he said rapidly, his moustache twitching as he talked. 'As you are well aware, the need for sedation in modern life has been gone into *ad nauseam* and I don't need to remind you about stress phenomena, anxiety states, tension...'

'Mr Piper!' I said.

'...what is needed more than anything is a sedative that is safe, effective, non-addicting, and with no after-effects. Now we have something that supplies all these qualities – and a few more besides...'

'Mr Piper, please!' My voice was hoarse. I was no match for Mr Piper. I sat down at my desk and put my head in my hands. The voice went on:

'...and then we have in one capsule a preparation which combines tetracycline and oleandomycin, a relatively new medium spectrum antibiotic with a range of activity similar to that of erythromycin...'

I must have dozed off for the next thing I heard was the word 'Golf.'

I sat up.

Mr Piper was placing the pile of literature on my desk together with two or three small samples.

'What was that you said?' I asked.

'Ah! About our lozenges. Soothing to the inflamed oral mucosa, non-toxic, pleasantly flavoured and acceptable to children.'

'No, not that!' I said, wondering if perhaps I had been dreaming. 'I thought I heard you say something about golf.'

'Yes,' he said. 'My firm is sponsoring a golf tournament for general practitioners. I was asking whether you were interested at all.'

'Good gracious, yes,' I said, my weariness completely disappearing. 'When is it?'

By the time Mr Piper left, I had waited so long for dinner that my hunger had evaporated.

Sylvia had already had her dinner, so she brought mine, which she had kept hot, on a tray into the morning-room. She was busily sewing name tapes on to numerous tiny garments which she had to take into the hospital with her when she had the baby.

'Why don't you finish it, Sweetie?' she asked as I put my knife and fork down, able to eat only very little.

'Too tired.'

'Poor Sweetie. Shall I get you something else?'

'No thank you, darling,' I yawned. 'Never mind. In twenty-five years' time perhaps I shall have someone to help me with the practice.'

'How do you mean?'

'Our one and only.'

Sylvia squinted at the needle she was threading.

'Oh! no!' she said. 'I don't think I'd like to see our daughter doing medicine. It's no life for a girl.'

'Daughter?'

'Mm,' she said, smiling. 'Blonde, with a pony-tail.'

I said nothing but picked up the newspaper and put my feet up on the mantelpiece.

Sylvia put her hands in her lap and looked at me.

'It's just sunk in,' she said. 'What you were saying about someone to help you with the practice? You're really banking on a boy?'

'Oh! no,' I said casually, keeping my face behind the paper. 'Whatever we have will be OK with me. After all, what does it matter?' I knew that that was how I *should* feel about it, but I didn't. I desperately and unreasonably wanted our only child to be a son. It was both stupid and unfair on Sylvia, and I was sorry that I had let her see how I felt.

'Look, darling,' I said, 'it really doesn't

mean a thing to me, as long as you and the baby are all right. Little girls are sweet and so are little boys.'

'I'd like to make you happy, Sweetie,' Sylvia said, 'since it's only going to be one.'

'You will, whatever it is,' I said firmly. 'Now, let's not be so stupid. After all, neither of us really minds, do we?'

'No,' Sylvia said, 'we don't mind a bit.'

But we did.

As often as I imagined a future with my son by my side I knew that Sylvia was still hoping for a daughter, although neither of us said anything. We always skated tactfully round the subject, referring to 'the baby,' until it came to problems like the paint.

'Pink!' Sylvia said. 'The very palest pink. Then we can have white curtains scattered with pink rosebuds.'

I looked at her in horror, offended at the thought of my son surrounded by pink rosebuds.

Together we both realised that we had given ourselves away. Sylvia recovered first.

'No,' she said, 'perhaps not. Pink, after all, is very ordinary. Had you anything particular in mind?'

I had visualised a manly blue. 'Not really. What about green?'

'Or yellow?' Sylvia said half-heartedly.

'Or grey?'

We settled for off-white on which I was to

stick black, silhouetted bunny rabbits.

In the surgery I asked for the loan of some equipment from patients who were in the building trade, and got ladders, planks, a pair of top quality brushes (known affectionately as Big Tom and Little Tom), a 'one-inch tool' for painting the architraves and a load of advice. After I'd 'rubbed down the winders,' 'filled me cracks,' and 'put on me undercoat,' according to instructions, I began to think I had missed my vocation!

All went well and I was extremely happy with my new-found occupation until my two jobs clashed, as they did at the most annoying and inconvenient moments. I had painted half the door which, for a professional finish, had to be done with the greatest concentration and in one particular way, when Timothy Jollop fell off his bike and presented a gaping knee to be stitched up; and I had my hands smothered in top-coat which had dripped from the ceiling when Mrs Barclay decided to have an attack of gall-bladder colic. Timothy had been too fascinated by the smudges on my face to cry, and Mrs Barclay in too much pain to notice the traces of Superlac White (semi-gloss) I left on her abdomen. I blamed a pyloric stenosis for 'tears' on the long wall, a second-degree burn for paint trodden into the staircarpet and ignorance for my failure to remove the light switch and door handles.

When it was all finished I was, not without reason I thought, proud of my handiwork.

'Think of the money we've saved,' I said to Sylvia as we stood in the doorway admiring the clean, bright room.

Sylvia said nothing but went to the stack of equipment I had piled in the middle of the room. Silently she held up the shirt, pullover, golf trousers, socks and shoes I had ruined with paint.

'Well,' I lied, 'I was going to throw them away, anyway.'

That night I nearly had to sleep among the bunnies I had so carefully stuck on to the walls.

After dinner we had gone into the nursery again to see how it looked by night.

Sylvia half-closed her eyes and stood in the middle of the room.

'We'll have the cradle there,' she said, pointing, 'the nursing-chair there and the baby bath there.'

'I don't know why you bother with all that,' I said, admiring my invisible brushwork. 'Most of the patients put the babies in an old laundry basket to sleep and bath them in the kitchen sink. I think I made a neat job of that awkward corner, don't you?'

When Sylvia didn't answer I looked at her. The tears were running down her face. In the next ten minutes I learned that I was not only heartless, thoughtless and stupid, but was accused of gross callousness and unwillingness to provide the most obvious essentials for our expected newcomer. One by one I managed to reclaim my hastily uttered words, and later, there among the hopping bunnies, was unconditionally forgiven.

I had long ago resigned myself to the fact that I had much to learn about women and marriage and had thought I was progressing quite nicely. Now I began to doubt if I had progressed much past Chapter One of the first volume.

That I was trying to economise by painting the baby's nursery was one particular indication of a new general trend. I had never been worried particularly about money. My father, medicine-mad and kind to the point of indulgence, had paid for my medical studies. In my hospital days, after I had qualified, the salary although ridiculously low had easily covered my carefree bachelor needs. In general practice, while I was still single, I was able to live comfortably. Marriage, however, seemed to put a different complexion on things. The practice, as practices go, was quite remunerative, but with my change of status certain things which before I had managed very nicely without seemed quite indispensable. My housekeeper and I, in the first year I was in practice, had been quite content to place, with mechanical regularity, buckets under the leaking fanlight every time it rained; we had ignored happily the ancient rumblings of the old-fashioned boiler in the kitchen which kept everything permanently smothered with a thin film of dust, and covered the milk bottles, in hot weather, with damp muslin. Sylvia, however, had a rooted objection to the almost permanent array of bowls and buckets in the corridor, could not live with grimy shelves, and said she didn't see why in the age of atomic power and the 'never-never' we had to act as though we were living in the back of beyond, with no main services. In consequence, we now had a leak-proof fanlight (whose repair incidentally had entailed extensive and costly adjustments to the flat roof), a shiny, dirt-free boiler in the kitchen and a fridge. Now we were going to have a baby and, judging by the terrifying number of garments, conveyances and coverings this as yet unborn child was going to need before it was anywhere near ready either to wear shoes or be educated, I thought it probably just as well we were not to have them in unlimited numbers. I was assured by my mother, Mrs Loveday, and by now keeping my eyes open to things other than the patients in the beds as I did my visits, that this state of affairs was quite normal. I had merely now to husband the resources which I had before let slip casually through my fingers, and make better use of the additional sources of income available to me as a general practitioner. In the interests of my growing family I got tough. By charging the patients for certificates for which I was entitled to a fee but about which I had never bothered, I collected enough shillings in a month to make me regret my previous slackness. By being more particular in notifying the Public Health authority of the immunisations and vaccinations which I did, I received the proper remuneration.

My efforts to provide for my family were not unaided. Most of the patients now knew about our expected increase and the news had affected them in various ways. The ladies on the Council estate knitted tiny garments and laid them diffidently on my desk; the ladies in the immediate vicinity knitted tiny garments and brought them to the front door, giving them to Sylvia together with advice based on their own, usually grisly, experiences about having babies. I became a likely target for what seemed to me the abnormally high proportion of gentlemen among my patients who sold insurance.

'But, Doctor, you must provide *now* for the future of your child...'

'Doctor, by paying these negligible premiums now, in twenty years...

'Doctor, you must insure your life. What would happen to your wife and child if...'

'This endowment policy, Doctor, will

bring you...'

'School bills, Doctor. And then you'll want him to have a university education...'

I listened carefully and felt the last remnant of my youth slip away. For at least an hour after one of these onslaughts I was quite depressed; my normally cheerful vision clouded with thoughts of what might happen if I dropped down dead, became maimed for life, got some incurable disease. I began to feel quite sorry for Sylvia and our poor, fatherless child.

They finally wore me down and, after much deliberation and evasion, I finally in self-defence provided myself with a small amount of life insurance; a policy which covered me in the event of a patient slipping on the floor of the waiting-room and breaking his leg; and another to insure myself against being struck by a golf ball. After which precautions I quickly forgot about the whole matter and almost regained my previous carefree attitude.

Another chance of extra income which I now agreed to tap was to administer dental gases for my friend Loveday. He had offered me the chance to do his gases when I first went into practice. I had refused because I had never particularly enjoyed giving anæsthetics. In view of my growing financial responsibilities, I decided that it was time I overcame my aversion. Loveday was surprised when I rang him up.

'But, my dear boy,' he said, 'you told me you'd hate to give my gases. What's made you change your mind?'

'LSD,' I said.

Loveday laughed. 'As a matter of fact, it's a good thing that you rang just now. My old anæsthetist is moving down to Devon. I was just about to ask that Compton chap if he did gases.'

'Good Lord!' I said. 'You can't do that!'

'All right,' Loveday said. 'I'll let you know when I have something.'

Two weeks later, his receptionist rang to say that Mr Loveday would like my help with a simple extraction.

Sixteen

It was on the day before the gold tournament arranged by Mr Piper's firm, Credo-Medicals Ltd, that I did my first gas for Loveday. In view of my performance, I was surprised that he ever asked me again to assist him. But then Loveday was a good sort. It wasn't that I was technically incompetent, although I hadn't given a dental gas since I had qualified, but just that on that first occasion I had been a little slow, with rather unfortunate consequences.

The patient was a middle-aged woman who had come to have four teeth extracted; three from one side of her mouth and one from the other.

With the patient made comfortable in the chair, I fitted the nasal mask and, switching on the nitrous oxide, instructed her to breathe deeply in and out through her nose. Gradually her breathing changed and became automatic. I glanced at her pupils, noted her colour and, when all seemed well, switched on the oxygen and told Loveday that I was all ready and that he could start the extraction.

For the removal of the first three teeth all went well. Loveday extracted them with expert speed and seemingly effortless dexterity. He then started to shift the gag that was holding the patient's mouth open, in order to expose the fourth tooth on the other side of the mouth.

The gag slipped and the woman's mouth half closed.

'I'll have the Mason's retractor,' Loveday said quickly, holding out his hand to me. 'You can hold her mouth open for me while I get this last one.'

I looked vaguely round the room, then noticed a tray of ferocious-looking dental instruments behind my left arm. While I pondered over the choice of weapons, trying to decide which particular retractor he was asking for, Loveday decided he couldn't wait. He put his fingers in the patient's mouth to hold the slipping gag in position, and quickly got hold of the last tooth.

I had just noticed the retractor I was sure he had asked me for when I saw him whip out the fourth tooth. At that moment the patient's jaws snapped shut. Unfortunately, Loveday still had his fingers in her mouth.

After muttering one extremely rude word, Loveday managed to restrain himself while the nurse helped the patient from the room. Then, gripping his bleeding fingers, he banged round the surgery, his seventeen stone rattling the equipment, swearing at me.

Apologising profusely, I offered him bandage and Elastoplast and even to stitch him up. When he'd exhausted his repertoire, the cream of which I had mistakenly thought I already knew by heart from the golf course, he said it wouldn't be necessary. He thanked me for helping him, and he even paid me.

I was surprised when he rang me two days later to say that he had a child with two teeth to extract, and could I give the anæsthetic. Considering that through me he had nearly lost three fingers, I thought it very decent of him. I gradually got to know what was required of me in addition to actually administering the gas, and by the time Loveday's fingers had completely healed we had formed a fine partnership.

When I came home for lunch and told Sylvia about my first unfortunate little episode with Loveday she said: 'That's funny!'

'I can't see anything very funny in nearly having your fingers bitten off,' I said.

'No, I don't mean that.'

'What *do* you mean?'

'You don't smell. When you used to give anæsthetics when you were working at the hospital, you smelt terrible for hours. I was almost anæsthetised when you kissed me.'

'This is different,' I said. 'We don't use any ether for dental gases. That's what I used to smell of at the hospital.'

Sylvia shuddered. 'Ugh. It was horrid. You were at the Chest Hospital then. Do you remember? I used to think you were wonderful in your white coat with your stethoscope dangling nonchalantly.'

'You were pretty wonderful too.'

Sylvia looked down at her bulging figure.

'I bet that good-looking driver wouldn't offer to run me home in the ambulance now!'

'He would get more than he bargained for if he did! Those were the good days,' I said, thinking of Sylvia waiting for me to come off duty in the doctors' sitting-room at the hospital; the dances, parties, walks on the Heath, dress shows when she was modelling.

She put her arms round me. 'These are better.'

'Are you sure?' I said anxiously, wondering if she still hankered after her old, glamorous life.

'Positive.'

Looking into her saucer-like blue eyes with their heartbreaking black lashes, I felt that she meant it. In spite of, or because of, her pregnancy, she was looking more beautiful than ever, and for the first time I was really able to believe that she was settling down and no longer yearned, or if so only very occasionally, for the cameras and the bright lights.

She seemed lately to be really enjoying her rôle of doctor's wife, and I suspected that it was because she was now getting to know the patients as more than just disembodied voices over the telephone. She met them when they called at the house for prescriptions, and kept up with their progress by asking me what my diagnoses were after I had been to visit them.

She seemed glad to be able to help when little Jenny swallowed a safety pin or pushed a bead up her nose while I was out on my rounds, and could advise with assurance what little Tommy should have for breakfast after a tonsillectomy. She also dealt in my absence with cuts and scalds, babies who had fallen out of cots or off draining boards, and aged relatives who had collapsed on the floor. She was able to assess the situation with confidence, reassure the panic-stricken callers and tell them exactly what to do.

Looking at her contented face, I felt sure that this way she would remain happy long after the bright lights would have dimmed.

The day of the Credo-Medical's golf tournament dawned bright and clear with a light spring breeze ruffling the newly leafed trees. Phoebe Miller had agreed to look after my patients for me for the rest of the day, so it was with an unusually light heart for a Tuesday that I got into the car after an early lunch and drove off towards the course where the tournament was to be played.

In the club house, Mr Piper, handlebar moustache bristling, was trying to get things organised.

'Aha!' he said merrily when he saw me. 'Good afternoon, Doctor, and a lovely afternoon it is too. I hope you know everybody here.'

I opened my mouth to answer when I saw his gaze slip behind me.

'Aha!' he said, walking towards the latest arrival. 'Good afternoon, Doctor. I hope you know everybody here.'

I looked round the little group. There were one or two GPs I knew only by sight, the pædiatrician from the local hospital, and the Medical Officer of Health. These last two, being not only lady doctors, but lady golfing doctors, were visions to behold. They may have been experts with the syringe and pretty nifty with their drivers, but I doubted if either of them would have known what to do with a lipstick. One was dressed in a suit, square-shouldered and looking as if it had survived at least one war, and had her greying hair pulled back into a tight bun, while the other had a full, blanket-like tweed skirt and heavy-knit jumper which did nothing for her already vast proportions, and to save herself the trouble of deciding what to do with her mousy hair she had cut it all off to within half an inch of her head. On acquaintance, both these ladies turned out to be utterly charming. They were not only sparkling conversationalists but played down to single figures. It was easy to forget their sartorial deficiencies.

In the corner of the lounge where we stood about diffidently, waiting for the latecomers, was a phone booth. Through the glass, I saw a young man lolling lankily against the door as he held the receiver to his ear. His back looked familiar. His front was even more so.

'Musgrove!' I shouted, going over to meet him as he came out. In spite of our well-meant promises, we hadn't contacted each other since Edinburgh. His glasses were still perched precariously on the end of his nose.

We shook hands. 'I saw you come in,' he said. 'I was just phoning my stockbroker.'

'Stockbroker?' I said. 'Have you come into money?'

'Not yet,' he said. 'I'm hoping to. The market looks fairly bright and I had a tip from one of my patients. It's a dead cert. And very hush-hush. I've just bought some shares and with a bit of luck I should have cleaned up a hundred pounds by the end of the week.'

'Good luck to you,' I said. 'If I had any spare cash I might have a bash myself.'

'My dear boy,' Musgrove put his arm round my shoulders, 'that's the whole beauty of it. You don't need a sou. You buy them on the account and sell them before the account has ended. That's if you've good reason to believe that they're going to go up in that time.'

'Suppose they go down?'

'That's a chance you've got to take. This patient of mine who gave me the tip has made a fortune on the Stock Exchange. I wouldn't just buy any old thing. That would be asking for trouble.'

'Have you made anything before by this method?'

'I could have made a tenner a few weeks ago but I hung on too long and then Eisenhower got a cold.'

'Eisenhower?' I said. 'What's he got to do with it?'

Musgrove looked pained at my ignorance.

‘Wall Street,’ he said, ‘dropped like a stone!’

‘I see,’ I said, although I didn’t really see at all.

‘Anyway,’ Musgrove said, ‘I had to try something. We’re expecting an increase in the family.’

‘So are we,’ I said.

‘Oh!’ Musgrove said despondently. ‘So you know all about that pram and nappies lark?’

‘And cots and baby baths.’

‘And bootees,’ Musgrove said. ‘As a matter of fact, my wife’s meeting me here later. It’s my half-day.’

‘You must come and have dinner,’ I said rashly. ‘Sylvia will be delighted. I’ve been going to ask you for ages. This is a splendid opportunity.’

‘You’d better ask your wife first,’ Musgrove said. ‘You can’t just appear with us. It might be chops, and that can be embarrassing. It happened to us once.’

‘Wait there!’ I said. ‘I’ll ring Sylvia.’

‘You’d better hurry. We seem to be nearly ready to start. They’re all going in to get changed.’

Iris answered the phone. I told her to tell Sylvia that I was bringing two guests home for dinner and that she should put on one of her specialities. Through the half-open door of the booth I heard Mr Piper say: ‘Come along, ladies and gentlemen, please!’ He was looking anxiously at his watch.

Iris was mumbling something about the dinner.

'I can't stop now, Iris. We're going to play off. Just give my wife the message.'

I joined the others in the changing-rooms and quickly got into my golf things. My golf trousers, which I never remembered to remove from my bag and which were permanently crumpled-looking, were now, in addition, spattered with white paint from the nursery walls. I tried to scrape some of it off, but since everyone seemed to be moving out, gave it up as a bad job and, pulling down my windcheater as low as possible in an attempt at disguise, followed them.

With the help of Mr Piper we made ourselves up into fours and started off. My first drive into the wind went straight as a die some two hundred yards and landed smack in the middle of the fairway. My mood set, I stepped jauntily off over the springy turf, holding my face up to the sun. For the first five holes I couldn't do a thing wrong. I cleared the hazards with an expertise wonderful to behold, and my chip shots on to the green were sheer poetry. On the sixth, which was a dog-leg, my ego was deflated. I sliced my drive and it landed in a patch of rough which lay by the side of the fourteenth green. Leaving the others on the fairway, I walked over to find it. It was just the wrong side of a prickly gorse bush. I had just made up my mind as to the best way to tackle it, and was taking my number eight iron out of my bag, when a voice behind me said:

'Oy!'

I looked round. A surly-looking greenkeeper was sweeping the fourteenth with his long besom.

'You'll 'ave to wait,' he said, looking at my crumpled, paint-spattered trousers. 'There's a tournyment playing. A doctors' tournyment.' There was admiration in his voice. 'You'd best let them play through.'

Ignoring him, my pride wounded, I addressed the ball. I missed it completely and had difficulty in disentangling my number eight iron from the gorse bush.

The rest of my game was only compensated for by the slap-up tea they provided back at the club house. Credo-Medicals did us proud with sandwiches, toast and jam and a large variety of cakes. Mr Piper made a little speech during which he said that he was sure the experiment had created much good-will for his firm, and that he would do his best to see that it was repeated. He presented cash prizes to the winners of the tournament – a small GP with a large tummy from Ealing, and the lady Medical Officer of Health – and to the rest of us he gave consolation prizes of golf balls bearing the name Credo-Medicals, lest we should forget. All in all, it was a most enjoyable afternoon.

Musgrove and his wife, a short, jolly, dark-haired girl, followed me home in the car. We had spent so long over our tea and talking to the boys in the clubhouse, that it was dinner-time when we pulled up outside my house behind a taxi. Out of the taxi, stepping carefully, came Sylvia. I remembered with horror that she had told me she was spending the afternoon with her mother and would be back late. In my mirror I watched Musgrove and his wife in their car behind me, looking forward expectantly, I was sure, since I had sung Sylvia's praises all through tea, to an exceptionally fine dinner. I was afraid they were going to be disappointed, but I had reckoned without Iris.

Lately we had noticed a change in Iris. She was still as cheerful and as willing as ever, but as the days grew longer and the weather warmer, we were reminded more and more frequently of Bridget. Iris let the milk boil over, the toast burn, and twice had sent me on visits to the wrong addresses. She blushed whenever she was spoken to, polished the red step with Brasso and forgot to unlock the waiting-room door until a large queue had formed down the garden path.

We were now to see that in spite of the recent extremely odd behaviour, she was still quite a girl.

When she let us all into the hall she was pink-cheeked and bubbling over with excitement. She wouldn't let Sylvia into the kitchen but said that dinner would be served in ten minutes. Since the most ambitious cooking she had done for us was to fry bacon or sausages or at the most put a joint in the oven, following Sylvia's precise instructions, we were both apprehensive and mystified. Iris was as adamant as she was excited, though, so we decided to let her get on with whatever she was doing.

The first surprise came before we even started to eat. Iris had set the table with our best mats and glasses and all the finery we kept for special occasions. Nothing had been forgotten and she had even lit two scarlet candles as she had seen Sylvia do.

Sylvia and I were practically dumb with astonishment as she served us with a dinner of *Oeufs en cocotte*, chicken marengo and lemon soufflé. It was Sylvia's favourite menu, but she couldn't have done it better herself. The Musgroves were most impressed. Mrs Musgrove talked babies with Sylvia and Musgrove initiated me into the mysteries of the stock-market.

They left at midnight, having admired my surgery and waiting-room, the matinée coats Sylvia had knitted and the bunnies I had stuck on the nursery wall.

In the kitchen Iris, tired but happy, was

drying the last of the coffee cups.

'Where did you get the chicken?' Sylvia demanded; 'we didn't have a thing in the house.'

'You said you could only fry!' I said accusingly.

'We only had three *cocotte* dishes left,' Sylvia said, 'and you produced four.' She sat down.

'Out with it, Iris!' I said. 'What's been going on?'

'Nothing really, Doctor,' she said. 'Nothing at all. Only when you phoned I tried to tell you there was only me in but you weren't listening. Well, I couldn't let you bring your friends home to cold beef from yesterday, with bubble and squeak. There wasn't enough, anyway. So I borrowed Hodge's bike and nipped down to the butcher's and bought a chicken, and they matched up the little dish at the china shop, and the lemons and the vegetables I brought in with me, and then I did it out of the book. I knew what it ought to look like, from watching.'

'What did you use for money?' Sylvia said.

'Oh! I drew out of my post office book. I was going to do that sweet with fresh pineapple we have sometimes, but they wanted ten and six for them. I told them it was a liberty, and took the lemons instead. It was all right?' she said anxiously.

Sylvia stood up and kissed her.

'Yes, Iris,' she said. 'It was more than all right. It was perfect.'

Seventeen

I discovered the reason for Iris' increasingly odd behaviour several weeks later, and in the public library.

The summer was now well advanced, the grass yellowing in patches from lack of rain, and Sylvia was getting near the end of her pregnancy. She found it very difficult to get about, was having frequent headaches, and spent much of her time resting. Iris took the double load of work, and the extra phone-answering, since Sylvia could not keep jumping up, willingly. She never complained, took wonderful care of Sylvia, and was very excited about the baby.

One Wednesday afternoon I called at the public library to borrow a book on the British countryside, a subject I had become interested in through driving through the glorious Surrey landscapes to visit Tessa Brindley in her country home. At one of the round tables in the Reference section, all dressed up in her 'half-day' clothes, sat Iris. She was reading a volume of the *Encyclopædia Britannica*, opened, I saw by looking over her shoulder, at a treatise on forestry.

I didn't disturb her but looked around for an explanation. Perched on the top of a ladder where he was putting away some books, I saw my patient, the good-looking Mr Westbeech, gazing down at the mop of red hair. I remembered his slipped disc, which Iris had helped me replace. Mr Westbeech noticed me looking at him and nearly fell off the ladder.

That night Iris came in as I was locking up.

'I didn't know you were interested in forestry,' I said casually.

She stopped dead, her key still in the door. 'In what?'

'Forestry,' I repeated. 'You were reading about it in the library.'

At the word library she turned scarlet.

'Oh!' she said.

'What's going on with you and Mr Westbeech?'

'We're going to get married!' Her voice was moony.

I was amazed.

'Mr Westbeech has asked you to marry him?' Iris nodded dreamily.

'How long has this been going on?'

'Ever since we met in the surgery.'

'Love at first sight?' I said.

'Love at first sight.'

'I thought you didn't want to get married because you didn't like to settle in one place. Itchy feet or something.'

'They've stopped itching.'

'I'm glad to hear it. I hope you'll be very happy.' A thought suddenly occurred to me. 'I suppose that means you'll be leaving us soon?'

Iris looked hurt. 'Not soon,' she said. 'I told you I'd stay until after the baby. We shan't be getting married for a year, anyway.'

There seemed nothing more to say, so I said goodnight.

Iris heaved a contented sigh and started up the stairs.

'Iris!'

'Yes, Doctor?'

'You've left your key in the door.'

She certainly had it badly.

In the night, Sylvia had her first false labour pains. The conversation, the first of many similar ones we were to have during the next couple of weeks, went something like this:

Sylvia: 'Ooh!'

Sylvia, a few minutes later: 'Ouch!'

Me: 'What is it, darling?'

Sylvia: 'Pains.'

Me: 'Where?'

Sylvia: 'In my back.'

Me: 'Do they go round to the front?'

Sylvia: 'Ooh! Yes.'

Me: 'Bad?'

Sylvia: 'Yes. I think I'm going to have the baby.'

Me (sleepily): 'It's too early.'

Sylvia: 'Ouch!'

Me: 'Are they getting worse?'

Sylvia: 'No. The same.'

Me: 'Well, try and go to sleep. Wake me up if they get any worse.'

Sylvia (drowsily): 'OK.'

The next thing I was aware of was the morning light streaming through the windows and Sylvia peacefully asleep at my side.

That day I was due to appear as an expert witness at the trial of Andrew Melrose for the murder of his two children. I hung about all day at the Old Bailey waiting for the case to come on, and then was not required: Andrew Melrose was found unfit to plead owing to insanity, and was sent to a criminal lunatic asylum.

Coming home in the car, I felt glad that he hadn't been found guilty and sentenced to hanging. It was true that his two small daughters were dead but nothing that now happened to their father could bring them back to life.

I had once visited a criminal lunatic asylum, having had special permission from the Home Secretary to accompany a psychiatrist friend of mine, and knew something of the life that lay ahead for Andrew Melrose.

I recalled the pleasant countryside we had driven through to get there and the stark forbiddingness of the high brick wall we found surrounding the place when we arrived.

The building was divided into blocks and each block was built round a central courtyard where the 'patients,' as they were now called, were exercised at various times of the day.

The worst cases were housed in what was known as the Refractory Block. Here the patients were kept under constant close observation, often in padded cells, and the 'nurses,' as the warders were now called, walked only in pairs.

There were lesser precautions in the Parole Block where the patients had opportunities to play billiards, watch television and even, once a year, to dance with the women inmates.

Everywhere we went, though, throughout the whole institution, there was the grim ceremony of unlocking every door we passed through and having it locked again immediately behind us. We trod softly down endless highly polished corridors in which there was no sound to be heard, no speck of dust to be seen, and completely bare of chairs or other furnishings.

The superintendent, a courteous old-school-tie type, strolled casually amongst the dangerous psychotic murderers, rapists, and child-killers, calling some by name and giving others a friendly nod and a smile. We asked him what this man's crime had been, and that one, and the man in the corner, but curiously enough the superintendent had forgotten. He now knew them only as his patients and they were all equal, not treated according to the severity of their crimes.

For the most part the patients took no notice of us. Some, lost souls, were walking tirelessly up and down, so many paces one way and exactly the same number the other; others shadow-boxed, and some passed away the days with endless skipping. These were the schizophrenics living in worlds of their own and completely out of touch with reality.

One seedy, pathetic-looking man approached us and asked us to smuggle a note to the Home Secretary asking for his release; another old man, knowing that we were doctors, introduced himself as a famous surgeon and rambled on about the hospitals he had worked in, mentioning the names of physicians and surgeons who had been well known but were long since dead.

It had been an interesting afternoon but we had both been glad when, outside at last, we headed for home through the sweet, free countryside. That tiny glimpse of life behind those high brick walls was something neither of us would easily forget. The grimness and the pathos left ineradicable imprints upon the memory.

To such an existence Andrew Melrose had now been committed.

Mental illness, even in its mildest form, is still, in the minds of the general public, a disgrace and a stigma, or at least a confession of moral weakness. Even in our enlightened day and age the patient and, even more strikingly, his relatives believe that admission to a mental hospital or even attendance at a psychiatric clinic is a fate to be avoided at all costs.

Mr Fletcher was a patient of mine who had had a short stay in a mental hospital and was determined not to go back. It was by playing on this knowledge that I was able on one occasion to help him.

He was a man of forty-five who was a mild depressive psychotic with an hysterical overlay. He often got very nervous about himself, and when he found life too much for him he retired into a hysterical coma from which it was often almost impossible to rouse him. Since he lived an impoverished existence in two rooms with a nagging and ailing wife, things got 'on top' of poor Mr Fletcher fairly often. At frequent intervals I was phoned up by various neighbours who had found Mr Fletcher collapsed in the street and apparently unconscious.

At one stage these attacks became so frequent that I had had to send him to a mental hospital where he was treated with modified insulin, sedation and suggestion. He seemed to be a lot better after this but always swore that he would never go back. I told him that if he kept fit it was unlikely that he would ever have to, and used it as a threat whenever he seemed likely to relapse into his anxiety state.

For a long time Mr Fletcher remained well.

One day, though, his wife rang me to say that he had been lying in bed for twenty-four hours, unrousable and unconscious. She had tried everything she knew but found him completely unresponsive, and she was at her wits' end. I said I would come to see him.

When I got there I found Mr Fletcher exactly as she had described him. Had I not known him of old I would have believed him to be deeply unconscious. When I tried to get some response from him I had no more success than his wife. Finally I picked up my case and said loudly:

'I'm sorry, Mrs Fletcher, but I shall have to get your husband admitted to hospital again.' To the prone figure in the bed I said equally loudly:

'Mr Fletcher, my surgery starts tonight at six o'clock. If I don't see you in the waiting-room by five past six I shall get on to the hospital to have you readmitted.' I then went out of the bedroom and slammed the door. Outside I crouched down and looked through the keyhole. For a while nothing happened, and I was just about to stand up because I was getting cramp in my legs, when Mr Fletcher sat up in bed.

'Blimey,' he said to his wife. ''E's a proper misery, ain't he?'

It is easy to blame the general public for the fear and trepidation with which they regard mental disorders and psychiatric treatment, but even the most broadminded and informed of doctors still consult their psychiatric colleagues about themselves or their relatives with some degree of stealth.

It is a situation badly in need of remedy and one in which I was very interested. I realised the importance of recognising mental disorders at an early stage, and it was something for which I tried to be constantly on the watch.

When I got back from the Old Bailey I rang the doctor who had been doing my emergency calls to say that I was back and would now take over, and went to find Sylvia to see what visits she had kept for me.

She was resting in the bedroom, and in the armchair by the side of the bed sat a formidable-looking woman, fat and middle-aged, wearing some kind of grey uniform with blue epaulettes. For a moment I couldn't think who she could possibly be, then I remembered that, on the advice of Humphrey Mallow, Sylvia had agreed to engage a maternity nurse to help her with the baby when she came out of hospital, as she would still have to take things very quietly. This, I realised, must be it.

Sylvia introduced me to Sister Hamble, then said: 'How was the Old Bailey?'

'Ooh!' Sister Hamble said. 'Has Daddy been a naughty boy?'

When I realised that she was talking to me I explained that I had not been a naughty boy but had been attending the trial of a patient of mine.

She smiled understandingly, revealing horse-like teeth.

'I've just been having a nice cosy chat with Mummy,' she said, 'and counting out our little vests and nighties. I'm sure we shall get on splendidly together, and if Daddy doesn't agree with my little ways he mustn't hesitate to say so.'

'Quite,' I said, and then to Sylvia: 'Can you tell me what visits I have still to do?'

Sister Hamble stood up. 'I'll go and have another little look at our bunnies on the wall,' she said, 'so that Mummy can talk to Daddy privately.'

When she had gone, after giving Sylvia a coy and cosy wink, I said:

'You haven't engaged her, have you?'

'Yes, I have,' Sylvia said. 'We've left it so late, you see, that she was the only one they had available. She has excellent references; some from people I know.'

'I don't care,' I said. 'I'm not having that woman in the house. "Has Daddy been a naughty boy?"' I said in disgust. 'I couldn't stand that for a fortnight.'

'I'm sorry, Sweetie,' Sylvia said, 'but there's absolutely no one else. I think they're all much the same, anyway.'

'Well, you'd better keep her out of my way,' I growled.

She gave me my visits, and a note which had been dropped in the door. It was from Archibald Compton and was a copy of the letter which the hospital had sent him about Renee Trotter. The poor girl had a carcinoma of the breast. If only she had consulted me about her symptoms instead of writing those idiotic letters, she would have been far better off.

There was a little tap at the door and a voice called: 'Have Mummy and Daddy finished?'

'God knows what she thinks we've been doing,' I said to Sylvia.

'Come in!'

'I always like to be understanding,' Sister Hamble said, when she was in. 'It makes for a happy atmosphere. I know because I've had to get on with so many Mummies and Daddies in my work.'

I left her to Sylvia and went down to the morning-room to make a phone-call. While I waited for them to ring me back I sat down in the armchair and picked up the *BMJ* to catch up with an article about combined prophylactics.

'There are three recognised ways in which the immunological response to a primary dose or course of an antigen may possibly be reduced,' I read; then there was a discreet tap at the door followed by the appearance of a grey, pudding-basin hat encircled by a blue hatband.

'I'll say goodbye, Daddy,' Sister Hamble said. 'It's a shame about our blood pressure, isn't it? We'll have to take great care of ourselves.'

'We do,' I said shortly.

'Oh! I'm sure we do, with a doctor for a daddy. It's a great pity we aren't having the baby at home. We do like to deliver our babies, you know,' she said hopefully.

'I'm sure we do.' I held out my hand. 'I'll say goodbye, Sister Hamble. I'm expecting an important phone-call.'

'Life and death?' she said dramatically, clasping her hands before her and leaning towards me.

'No. As a matter of fact, it's from my stockbroker.'

She pulled on her leather gloves.

'Ah!' she said. 'Daddy wants to get out of the market while the going's good. We're going to have a nasty little slump.'

I stared at her. She was half out of the door. She waggled two fingers at me.

'Bye-bye, Daddy,' she chirruped. 'Look after Mummy.'

I stared at the door which she had slammed after her. The phone started to ring shrilly. I picked it up, almost mesmerised by the voice I heard repeating in my ears: 'We're going to have a nasty little slump.'

Pulling himself together, 'Daddy' said hallo to his stockbroker.

Eighteen

Encouraged and convinced by Musgrove I had, after giving the matter a great deal of thought, decided to speculate on the Stock Market in an effort to increase my practically non-existent capital.

On the day that Sister Hamble had predicted a 'nasty little slump' I had invested in a modest hundred shares, as advised by Musgrove's patient-in-the-know, and hoped to get out with a nice quick profit before the end of the account. I made up my mind to sell the shares again on the day that our baby was due to arrive, and as they had risen steadily since I had held them, I looked forward to reaping my little windfall and confronting Sylvia with my successful *fait accompli*.

On the actual day our child was due to be born, however, something happened which left me no time to look after Sylvia, and even less to think about the Stock Market.

Tessa Brindley committed suicide.

I hadn't left Sylvia alone for more than an hour or so at a time for the past week, but when the call came from H H Brindley just as I was finishing my morning's surgery, there was nothing else I could do.

HH sounded desperate and shaken.

'Summat's up with our Tessa,' he said. 'Housekeeper's just phoned from the country to say she's taken ill. You'll come right away, won't you?'

It would take most of the morning to get to Brindley Manor and back.

'What seems to be the matter?' I said.

'She couldn't tell me nowt,' Brindley said. 'She were too agitated. Only said to hurry.'

I wondered if Sylvia was going to go into labour that day, then remembered my promise to HH to look after Tessa, 'no matter what.'

'All right,' I said. 'I'll be down as soon as I can.'

I rang Phœbe Miller, who agreed to do any urgent calls which couldn't wait until I got back, and went to break the news to Sylvia.

'I'll be back as soon as I can,' I said, 'but just in case anything happens I'll leave you the number of the ambulance.'

'Sweetie,' Sylvia said from the kitchen table where she was sitting down topping and tailing gooseberries, 'please don't worry about me. I feel absolutely fine today, and in any case most women don't have their husbands hanging around waiting for the first pain. They all seem to get themselves to hospital in time.'

'A friend of my mother's had hers in the street,' Iris said.

I glared at her.

'I don't want you to leave her, Iris,' I said. 'Not for a moment.'

I wrote Humphrey Mallow's telephone number in ink on the kitchen wall above the telephone and made Sylvia promise to phone him if she had any pains at all. There seemed nothing else to do since I couldn't ensure that she didn't start going into labour before I got back, so I repeated the emergency drill to her and Iris, and left.

Feeling depressed and miserable, I drove off through the morning traffic, taking it as a personal affront every time the signals turned to red or I was held up in a stream of cars. I could think of nothing but Sylvia standing in the doorway to see me off, large but beautiful, and telling me not to worry.

On the main by-pass I put my foot down and, ignoring the protestations of the car, overtook everything in sight. By the time I reached the winding stillness of the summer lanes I was feeling a little better. With any luck I should be back before lunch and there was, after all, no reason why our baby should choose to appear on this particular morning. From my experiences with my patients, I knew that it was rare for them to turn up exactly when they were expected.

Creeping round the hairpin bends and bouncing sickeningly over the little hump-backed bridges, I wondered what could be the matter with Tessa. I had been visiting her at regular intervals and her health had been exceptionally good. She had settled down to country life and spent the days peacefully thinking only of her Tony and the child which she was going to have. She still hadn't told her father exactly who Tony was and, according to Tessa, he had stopped asking her. HH had said nothing more about the matter to me.

Brindley Manor was a glorious Georgian house in a breathtaking setting. It lay at the foot of three gently undulating hills which protected it from the Surrey breezes and provided a backcloth for the magnificent grounds in which a miniature lake and a superb rose garden were only two of the attractions.

The house itself, beautifully furnished by one of the foremost interior decorators, had a concealed television screen in every room, and at least three cocktail bars. The whole thing was extremely sumptuous, if lacking in individual taste and personality.

When I arrived at the front door at the end of the mile-long, yew-lined drive, I found that HH in his maroon Rolls had beaten me to it.

He was up in the bedroom trying to rouse Tessa.

'It's not a bit of good, sir,' the housekeeper was saying. 'I've tried cold water and even smacking her poor face. I think ... I think ... she's...' She hid her face in her apron and ran from the room.

There was no doubt. Tessa Brindley, her ash-blonde hair streaming over the green and white striped pillow with its starched, frilly edge, was dead.

I sent HH out of the room while I had a look at her. I thought she must have been dead for quite a few hours but could find no evidence as to why she had died.

The room, a pretty young girl's room, appeared to be in perfect order. On a frilly-skirted dressing-table were Tessa's photographs. Her mother, her father, two or three girl friends, a group of boys and girls in bathing costume by the sea; they looked as if they were having a good time. On a chair lay her clothes, neatly folded; by the bed, on the small table, was a book of short stories, the place marked with a piece of blue ribbon. There was nothing to suggest that Tessa had taken her own life.

Downstairs in the lounge filled with chintz and sunlight, H H Brindley sat with his head in his hands.

'I'm so sorry,' I said. 'I shall have to ring the Coroner's Officer. I can't find any reason for her death.'

There was no reply. The house was silent except for the sobbing of the housekeeper coming from the kitchen.

I wasn't sure whether he had heard me.

'Mr Brindley,' I said. 'I would like to ring the Coroner's Officer.'

He still said nothing and didn't move.

'Would you like me to get you a drink?' I said.

He raised his head and stared straight at me without appearing to see me.

'I did it,' he said, and his voice was rough. 'I killed her with me own hands.'

I poured him some brandy and put the glass into his hands.

'Look,' I said, 'you'd better tell me what's been going on.'

'I never thought she meant it,' he said. 'I

never thought she meant it. Not our little Tessa.'

Suddenly I remembered Tessa's threat to take her own life if ever HH tried to find out who was the father of her child.

The memory made me grow cold, and at that moment I don't think I could have borne to be H H Brindley.

'You found Tony, then?' I said, knowing what the answer would be.

'Aye,' he said, 'I found Tony all right. I wanted to do the right thing by our Tessa.' He drank a little of his brandy, spilling some on his suit. He didn't bother to remove the staining drop.

'It took me a long time,' he said, 'but I found him. He's a journalist, a nice enough chap but very ordinerry.'

I remembered Tessa's accurate description of how Tony would appear to her father.

'It was only three days ago I actually met him,' he went on, still staring straight ahead of him like a man in a trance. 'Some place in Chelsea he lives, with his wife and two children. I knew he worked late on Thursdays at the paper so I called at the flat before he was due to arrive. I wanted to see for meself what the position was. It's not much of a place but smartened up a bit with window boxes like, and they live on the top floor. 'Is wife was in; one of these blue-stockings with great thick glasses and an

Oxford accent.

'I told 'er I'd come to see 'er husband. She never asked me what about but said I could come in and gave me a drink – it looked like it was the last of the sherry – and told me to make meself at 'ome like. It were a right difficult place to do that in, even if I hadn't been bubbling over. There was nothing but bookcases and yards and yards of books, and the carpet was frayed and there were no springs in the sofa. She was reading some great book or other, but I reckon she'd o' been better off washing curtains or summat.

'When she heard her husband cooee up the stairs, she yelled for him to bring coke bucket and to hurry 'cause he had a visitor. I 'eard him ask if 'is dinner was ready, and she said it were a kipper and she were just going to put it under grill.

'When 'e came in 'e'd been drinking. 'E set down coke bucket, slapped me on back and asked me who I was.

'"I'm Tessa's dad," I said, reckoning it would wipe the smile off 'is face. It did. 'E got quite pale and shut the door.

'"I would 'ave been home before," 'e said, "but I had a couple o' beers with the boys."'

I interrupted him to give him a little more brandy. He appeared not to notice.

''E didn't deny anything nor try to get out of it,' HH said, 'I'll give the lad that. I thought that when I set eyes on the man who ruined our Tessa I'd strangle him with me own two hands but I did nothing of the sort. I listened to what 'e had to say and ended up by feeling sorry for him. 'E didn't love 'is wife, he told me. She were too busy reading books, improving her mind and the like to look after him or the children properly, but 'e was crazy about those two kids. The pair of them 'adn't lived as man and wife since the youngest was born because she only believed in spiritual love or some such tommy-rot, but 'e couldn't run out and leave 'er with the kids.'

To me it sounded a pretty sordid story; the frustrated husband who had taken a pretty mistress to satisfy his appetites.

'I know what you're thinking,' HH said, 'because that's what I thought meself, but it's not quite like that. That boy was crazy about our Tessa, was nearly mad with worry over what had happened, but thought that his first duty lay to his two children. 'E knew I had plenty of brass and could look after Tessa, he said, but there was no one but 'im to look after his kids. 'E knew what 'e'd done and said no one was to blame but himself. 'E 'adn't dreamed that anyone like our Tessa could exist, and when he met her 'e was so bowled over he lost 'is 'ead.'

HH took a drink of the brandy I had put into his glass.

'He didn't say nowt but I reckon our Tessa

encouraged him. The more I spoke to him the more I took to him. Straightforward chap he was and dead set on sticking by his kids. 'E knew that if 'e told 'is wife everything and she divorced 'im, she would be given the custody of them. 'E said she wasn't fit to look after them as all she ever thought about was books.'

'Did you tell Tessa you'd been to see Tony?' I asked.

There were tears in HH's eyes as he said: 'It was such a right mix-up I clean forgot to tell the lad not to mention it. It wasn't till the housekeeper phoned this morning that I thought Tessa might have been serious about taking 'er life if I tried to find Tony. She's seemed so happy down here these last weeks I reckoned that was all just talk because she was worried, to begin with. I should have remembered she was a Brindley. We don't say nothing lightly; none of us.'

'We still don't know that she's taken her own life,' I said.

'You may not,' he said, 'but I don't need no Coroner's Officer to tell me about our Tessa. How she's done it I don't know, but she's done it.'

I phoned the local police station for the Coroner's Officer. It was well on into the afternoon before he arrived.

When he came he found an empty bottle

of sleeping tablets outside Tessa's bedroom window where it had been thrown into the wisteria. It looked as if she had taken them from the housekeeper's room and swallowed more than half the bottle in a successful attempt to end her own life and that of the child she was carrying.

This evidence didn't surprise Brindley who still sat, a broken man, in the chintz armchair. He remained unmoved when he was told there would have to be a post-mortem and an inquest.

When the Coroner's Officer left, taking with him the notes he had made about his findings, the house returned to its morning stillness.

When a bell rang, shattering the silence, I went to answer the front door.

On the doorstep stood a young man in a grey flannel suit. Over his shoulder I saw the battered drop-head coupé in which he must have arrived. He was good-looking but his face was tired.

'Mr Brindley?' he said.

I held the door open for him to come in. There was no doubt in my mind who he was.

In the lounge where bars of sunlight now striped the thick green carpet, the young man stood awkwardly.

HH glanced once at him, then sank his head again on to his hands.

The young man took an envelope from his pocket.

'I had a letter from Tessa,' he said, speaking to Brindley who took no notice, 'saying goodbye. I realised suddenly that I couldn't let her go, so I told my wife everything. I should have done it before. She wants me to divorce her as she's found a don who thinks, as she does, that love should be spiritual. She doesn't even want the children.'

H H Brindley didn't move. The young man looked at me as if for help, then struggled on addressing the motionless figure in the armchair.

'I came straight away,' he said. 'I know how you must feel about me and that it should all never have happened, but I'll make it up to her, I promise.'

He took a step towards Brindley and said clearly: 'I want to marry Tessa.'

It seemed an age before HH lifted his head from his hands and looked at the young man with red-rimmed eyes in which there was hatred only for himself.

'Tessa's dead,' he said. 'She killed herself.'

There was nothing more that I could do. I picked up my case and left, leaving together the two men who had loved Tessa Brindley more than anything else in the world.

Nineteen

On the gravel drive the shadows of the yew trees were lengthening. The countryside seemed not so beautiful and the winding lanes frustrating rather than picturesque. Each time I looked in the driving mirror I saw the face of Tessa Brindley, and ringing in my ears was her gay laugh remembered from the night she came to dine with us. I remembered the look of adoration in Faraday's eyes, and Tessa's frank gentleness on the occasions when I had seen her professionally.

It was a long time since I had seen suicide by an overdose of barbiturates, although at one time in my life they were almost an everyday occurrence. But then I hadn't known them personally and full of life as I had known Tessa.

My first hospital job after qualifying had been as Casualty Officer at a small hospital. The surrounding district was one inhabited, in addition to the more conventional residents, by a vagrant population of artists, writers, musicians and refugees from a variety of persecuted countries. This shifting band of wanderers lived for the most part in bed-and-breakfast vacancies where unsympathetic landladies, loneliness and frustration of their artistic abilities did nothing to increase their happiness. For the most part they had no families. They walked alone, drank rivers of coffee over midnight sessions of intellectual and earnest discussion, loved and lost. When the loneliness or the longing for home or the meanness of the landlady became more than they could bear, they tried to put an end to it all. Sometimes they were successful; often they were not.

Usually they were young men and girls in the very prime of their lives. If they were brought in dead it was my job to go out to the ambulance to confirm this and they were taken straight to the mortuary. Sometimes they were blue because they had sought oblivion by hanging themselves; often they were sodden from drowning. Some of the attempts at suicide were merely hysterical gestures, to 'show' a lover who had jilted them or bring remorse to a friend who had treated them badly. They didn't expect to die but often did.

Those who wished to make really sure took enormous doses of barbiturates or gassed themselves, taking extensive precautions to see that no gas escaped and no fresh air entered the room.

If they had been found before they were quite dead we applied artificial respiration, oxygen and stimulants by injection. Sometimes, in cases of barbiturate poisoning, they were unconscious for four to five days, but we kept them alive with intravenous fluids, powerful stimulants to counteract the drugs they had taken, and large doses of penicillin to prevent them getting infected lungs and pneumonia. It took me a long time to get used to the fact that those patients who recovered because of unceasing efforts on the part of doctors and nurses usually came back a month or two later, having made doubly sure that this time the job was not botched.

That district had one of the highest suicide rates, and many of the victims had been as young and as beautiful as Tessa. I hadn't forgotten them, and it would take me a long time to forget her.

As I drove due west into the sun, my windscreen a resting place for dirt, dust and numerous summer insects, I looked out for a telephone box. It had been impossible to phone home from Brindley Manor as HH had put through a call to his wife who was holidaying in Majorca, and was waiting for her to ring him back. I had been away far longer than I had expected, and was now anxious to make sure that Sylvia hadn't started to have the baby.

I stopped outside a phone box in a deserted road. The number rang for a long time during which I noticed in the little mirror that I had two grey hairs, then Iris answered. I asked her if Sylvia was all right.

'I'm awfully glad you've rung,' she said. 'She hasn't said anything but she's gone to lie down.'

'Let me speak to her.'

'OK. Hold on.'

'And, Iris...' But she had gone. I heard the mocking burr of the dialling tone against my ear. We had either been cut off or Iris, dreamy as she was with love, had replaced the receiver. In any event, I had no more change.

Back again in the car I started the engine, intending to drive the two or three miles into the next village, which was Hoxley, where I would be able to get some change and phone again. I had just put her into gear when there was a horrible 'clank' which seemed to shake the whole car, then another clank, followed by a continuous, harsh grating noise. The car refused to move. I tried again with exactly the same result. As George Leech had prophesied, something drastic seemed to have happened and it couldn't have happened at a worse moment. Wishing that I had listened to him and invested in a new car, I got out and started walking down the hot, tarry lane towards Hoxley. A few cars passed me but took no notice of my raised arm and pointing thumb asking for a lift. Remembering the number of times I had sailed merrily by hitch-hikers, I couldn't blame them. After I must have walked a hot and tedious mile, pressing myself against the prickly hedge every time I heard the sound of an engine, I was picked up by the matey driver of a brick lorry and dumped outside Hoxley's one-eyed, sleepy-looking garage.

The garage owner, in greasy overalls, said 'Ooh' and 'Aah' and shook his head when I asked him if he could go and have a look at my car, abandoned outside the phone booth. There was only him there, he said, since his mate was out and he had no one to leave in charge. My explanation that I was a doctor, and that I thought my wife was going to have a baby any minute, left him cold. When I took out my wallet, he said well he might just nip down on his motorbike to oblige. I promised to look after the garage for him while he was gone, if he didn't mind me using his telephone, and for a small sum the bargain was sealed.

From the tiny cupboard of an office surrounded by bottles of chrome-cleaner and shiny tins of One-Step polishes, I dialled my home number. I heard the ringing tone which jangled on and on and on, but there was no reply. I got hotter and hotter with agitation. I dialled the number again and asked the operator to test the line. There was definitely no reply.

I rang Humphrey Mallow's number. His secretary said he was out. He had gone to the hospital for an emergency Cæsarian. No, she didn't know who the patient was and she hadn't spoken to my wife, but then she'd only just come back from delivering some X-rays for Mr Mallow. Why didn't I phone the maternity hospital if I thought she might have been admitted? I phoned the hospital. Sister said no, my wife hadn't rung to say she was coming in, and Mr Mallow wasn't in the building as far as she knew.

I couldn't think what might have happened to Sylvia but my imagination was running riot. I stared with impotent hatred at the receiver, gave the sister the name and number of the garage in case she should get any news, and told her that my car had broken down and that I was likely to be there for some time. She promised to ring me if she heard anything from Sylvia. Half-heartedly I tried my home number again. I hung on listening to the monotonous burr-burr until I could no longer stand the heat in the little glass-fronted box on which the sun was beating down, then I replaced the receiver.

I had no customers in the garage, and waited impatiently for the owner to come back. When he did, he put away his motor-bike with maddening slowness and wiped his forehead, which was beaded with sweat, on a filthy black rag. He shook his head sadly.

'You can say goodbye to that little lady,' he said. 'Reckon it's your crown wheel and pinion gone. Cost more to put right than what it's worth. Mind you,' he said, warming to his theme, 'I'm not saying they wasn't a very good little car in their day, but if you don't mind my saying so, Doctor, you didn't oughter've kept 'er so long; not in your line of business you didn't. You might 'a been lucky an got another coupla thousand out of 'er. On the other 'and you might 'a 'ad a narsty haccident.'

I didn't mind him saying what George Leech had said long ago.

'What about a taxi?' I said. 'Or a car I can hire? Anything at all. I have to get home in a hurry.'

He looked at his watch.

'Reckon Alf'll be back inside ten minutes,' he said.

'Who's Alf?'

'My mate. He's out taking a lady to the airport. He'll run you home, Doctor, Alf will.'

'You don't think he'll be more than ten minutes?'

'Never known Alf miss his tea yet.'

'All right,' I said, and, perching myself on an empty oil drum, settled down to wait for Alf.

'There's a caff up the road,' the garage man said. 'Joe's place.'

I shook my head.

He found another oil drum and, rolling it over to where I was sitting, made himself comfortable beside me.

'Fag?' he said sociably, taking from his overalls some cigarette papers and a tin of tobacco.

'No thanks.'

After a few minutes of intense concentration the cigarette was ready, and he was running his tongue along the length of the paper. To my surprise, the cigarette, prepared by his filthy paws, was still white.

After he had lit it, taken a long draw and removed a few loose shreds of tobacco with great ceremony from his lips, he said:

'See my head?'

I looked at him without encouragement, wondering where Sylvia could possibly be and what was happening while I was stuck on an oil drum in a one-eyed garage.

'Wouldn't think it 'ad a steel plate inside, would yer?' He paused for an exclamation of surprise which was not forthcoming. 'It 'as, though. And take a butcher's at me ear.' He stuck his greasy mop of hair, which all but hid a disfigured ear which had been the subject of plastic repair, under my nose.

'Battler Britain,' he said proudly. 'Tail-end Charlie. Bang-bang-bang-bang-bang.' He aimed an imaginary gun at the two petrol pumps. 'Lucky to be 'ere. Came down in the drink. Never did like the water...'

I looked at my watch. I would give Alf five more minutes, then walk up the road and try to hitch a lift.

The garage man droned on about his wartime experiences. Going through in my mind every obstetric disaster in the book, I heard only the odd word. 'East Grinstead ... skin grafts ... got me ticket ... met the wife ... always been keen on cars and kits ... bought this little place with me gratuity ... pension.'

At every sound of an engine I pricked up my ears.

When at the end of ten lengthy minutes, there was still no sign of Alf, I got off my oil drum.

'Look,' I said, 'I'm just going to try my home number again and if your pal Alf hasn't turned up by then I won't wait. I'll start walking and see if I can hitch a lift.'

I was halfway across the oily-smelling yard towards the little office when I heard the deep thrum of an approaching engine. I waited as it drew nearer and louder, and jumped back as the familiar long snout of a gleaming black Allard swung into the garage, missing me by inches.

A yellow-gloved hand preceded a head of slicked-back black hair out of the window.

'Hop in!' Archibald Compton said.

The garage man was staring with open-mouthed admiration at the car.

The door swung open and in a daze I accepted the invitation.

'Hurry up, man! The membranes have just ruptured but she's doing fine. I don't suppose you'll have an increase in the family before we get there.'

'Sylvia?' I said stupidly.

Compton nodded and revved up. I shut the door just in time. With his yellow gloves chasing each other round the wheel, he swung the long black nose round the petrol pumps and with an urgent boom-boom-boom we were off down the road, leaving behind the garage man and a cloud of dust.

'I might as well explain,' Compton said, driving with terrifying expertness and keeping his foot well down on the accelerator until the trees flashed by so fast they appeared planted only about two inches apart, and the engine sounded like a child crying.

'I'd be glad if you would.' I stretched my legs out in front of me on a level almost with my body from the low-slung seat.

We curved sickeningly round a bend. 'I was in Sister's office at the hospital when you phoned,' Compton said. 'I'd been to visit a patient of mine who's just had a mis. Just after you rang off your wife was admitted, and Sister was so cross that she hadn't known a minute or two before while you were still on the line, that she told me the whole story.

'She wanted to phone you back and tell you your wife had just come in, but I wouldn't let her. I knew you'd only be worried at being stranded here, so I thought I'd pop down myself. I had nothing else to do and I used to live down this way so I know all the short cuts.'

'I hardly know what to say,' I said. 'It's terribly decent of you to go to so much trouble.'

'No trouble at all. Any excuse for a drive. I can never let her have her head at home. I know what it's like, anyway, when you're expecting a first baby. Especially when you start thinking what could happen.'

'Did you see Sylvia?'

'Yes. The membranes had ruptured but she had a long way to go yet. She was still smiling. Your maid brought her in by ambulance.'

All the things I had said or thought about Archibald Compton went crawling round in my head. This was the first time I had exchanged more than two or three words with him, and I was unable to detect the ogre who I imagined had come to gobble up my practice.

'How are you doing in the practice?' I

asked, because I knew that he would probably not bring the subject up before the surly brute he must imagine me to be.

'Not too badly. I have enough patients to keep me busy, which was the general idea. I've often wanted to come and apologise for practically squatting on your doorstep, but up till now the past was too close for me to be able to talk about it with any confidence that I could finish the conversation. I only chose that spot so that I could be near my wife's family.'

'The Harts?' I said, knowing now why they had gone off my list.

'Yes. I've no family of my own. You don't need to worry, anyway; I've no intention of trying to build up a large practice. I shall most probably emigrate in a year or so.'

I pictured his life since the tragedy which had taken his wife and child. The loneliness with too many hours to think, the sudden necessity for reorientation to bachelordom again, the solitary lunches in the suburban cafés; my unfriendliness. I had thought him brash, conceited; he had probably only been unhappy.

'Do you want a boy or a girl?' Compton asked, changing the subject.

'I don't mind at all,' I said, and to my surprise I found for the first time that I really didn't mind. Whether it was because I had so much and Compton so little, I don't know, but I knew now that I would be equally thrilled about either.

We reached the hospital in twenty-five minutes from leaving Hoxley.

As I got out Compton said: ‘I’ll do your calls for you tonight and tomorrow. Stay with your wife.’

My answer was lost in the roar of his engine, and as he snaked away all I could see through the back window was a flash of yellow glove. For the first time I felt no envy; only shame.

Twenty

In a small room which looked out on to the well of the hospital Sylvia was lying placidly in bed, timing her pains.

‘Sweetie!’ she said, holding out her arms, ‘I was so worried. What happened to the car?’

‘It broke down,’ I said. ‘It looks as if we’ll have to get another one, but never mind that now. Are you all right?’

‘I’m fine. I just sent for the ambulance as you said. Iris came in with me; she really is sweet, that girl, and now she’s gone back because of the telephone.’

‘And the pains?’

'A little worse than they were but not too bad. There's nothing to it. I don't know why everyone makes such a fuss.'

I kissed her for her optimism.

'What was the matter with Tessa Brindley?'

I took her hand. 'Nothing very much.'

'You were so long.'

'I had to stay there for a while.'

'Is she all right now?'

'Yes,' I said, 'she's all right now.'

I waited while Sylvia struggled through a pain. Out of the window I could see directly into the ward opposite. A nurse was arranging some flowers; there were red blankets on the two neat rows of beds.

'Was it bad?'

Sylvia shook her head and lay back to rest.

A nurse came in with a covered surgical trolley. She showed me all her teeth.

'We'll wait in the waiting-room now, shall we?'

'Don't go, Sweetie!' Sylvia said.

'I'll come back soon.'

'Don't leave it too long. Your son might have arrived.'

'Darling,' I said, 'it takes a long, long time.'

Downstairs I rang up George Leech about a new car. He spent nearly ten minutes saying, 'I told you so,' when I explained what had happened to the old one, then he said it was fortunate that I'd phoned up at that moment as he had the Very Thing. As well as being the Very Thing, it was Very Heavy on petrol and Very Expensive. I told him to forget it and to find me a small saloon within my price range. 'Oh!' he said, why hadn't I told him I was thinking along those lines. He had the Ideal Car. The only trouble was that it was plum-coloured and he didn't know if I cared for plum. I settled for the Ideal Car in plum.

Sister told me that Humphrey Mallow was on his way. The nurse was still busy with Sylvia so I left a message that I would be back in half an hour and went out to find something to eat. At the Brindley's I had completely forgotten about lunch and now my rumbling stomach reminded me that I had had nothing since breakfast.

At a grubby café, since there seemed nothing better in the neighbourhood, I served myself with beans on toast, a dejected salad and coffee turned grey by the strip lighting, and sat down to eat it at a table littered with dirty crocks and a half-eaten sandwich left by the last customer.

By the time I got back to the hospital Sylvia was working in earnest to produce our baby. I was too upset by the sight of her pain to stay with her, and she was quite glad to see me go so that she could get on with it. I had a word with Humphrey Mallow who had just arrived, then went downstairs to find the waiting-room. I looked through an old *Tatler*, a motor magazine and the *Saturday Evening Post* before I realised that I wasn't taking in a single word that I read.

It was a long night. I suppose that once or twice I must have dozed off although I wasn't conscious of doing so.

I made frequent journeys down the silent corridors lined with the flowers that had been put out for the night to Sylvia. She was too busy to notice me. From time to time Humphrey Mallow came down to tell me how she was getting on.

'Will it be before breakfast?' I croaked, my voice hoarse with anxiety, on one occasion.

'It depends on what time you have your breakfast.'

'It seems to be a rather prolonged first stage, doesn't it?'

'Not at all. Not at all. Why don't you go home to bed? I'll look after your wife and let you know the minute anything happens.'

But I couldn't go home. Although I had brought some hundreds of babies into the world myself and watched many others being born, this was different. It was terrible.

Night Sister brought me cups of tea and bright layman's talk about how 'nicely' Sylvia was doing, and that 'it shouldn't be long now.' When I asked her if she was fully dilated she didn't answer, but I didn't really want to know.

I had plenty of time to think. Most of the time I thought about Sylvia, but the image of Tessa Brindley, her face still, but her pretty hair shining with life, kept creeping into my mind. Her death seemed so unnecessary. I thought of all the patients in my practice who had to die before their time and didn't want to: a young schoolboy with leukæmia, a middle-aged woman trying to cling to life long enough to see her first grandchild born, pitting her will against the malignant, inexorable growths in her chest; the small baby with congenital heart disease who had hardly lived. I almost hated Tessa for throwing away the gift to which so many people pinned their hopes through pain and illness, poverty and despair. Her death must have been in the order of things, but in spite of her wrongdoings the judgement seemed harsh.

Sister rushed by and said: 'The head's appeared. Won't be long now.'

A prickle of excitement went through me. I was grateful to Humphrey Mallow for staying with Sylvia. It was common practice for consultants to arrive only to deliver the babies. I felt sorry for keeping him from his bed, as my patients so often felt sorry for me. As an obstetrician, he probably spent more hours out of bed than I, although his life in general was far more leisurely.

For the fourth time I tried to count the elusive roses on the curtains and thought that while the whole world was tending towards automation, the GP's job remained a twenty-four-hour one, and made demands upon us which had no parallel in any other profession. Rain, hail, snow or fog, we were on duty day and night responsible for our own deputising arrangements. We were presumed to be fit at all times and mentally alert, even though after several hectic days and possible night calls we might be at the point of exhaustion. Occasionally at this low ebb, with brain fuddled from lack of sleep and body aching with weariness, we were called upon to make a decision on which a patient's life might depend. Such was the life I had chosen, and there was little in it of the old-time drama. With antibiotics and steroids, with hospitals, ambulances and auxiliary services at the end of the telephone, the minor, kitchen-table surgery, the pneumonia crises and the difficult births were a thing of the past.

A large proportion of my work was a direct result of the intense pressure of modern life, the speed of movement and action, the altered social standards. I dealt with demands for stimulants, the fight against depression and insomnia, the craze for slimming and tranquillisers. I still had to leave my warm bed in the night, though, and still had to turn out whether I liked it or not. The profession had, now that medicine was no longer a mystery, lost a lot of its glamour, but none of its arduousness. I felt sorry for myself but knew I would never find such contentment doing anything else; I grumbled at the hours, the Health Scheme, the stupidity of the layman, but I was never bored because I never, ever, had a dull moment; I knew that according to statistics I might drop dead of coronary thrombosis in early middle-age, yet I didn't care. I loved my work – a state of affairs which was becoming, according to what my patients told me, increasingly rare.

I must have hypnotised myself to sleep counting roses instead of sheep because, when I opened my eyes, the birds were singing and the first light creeping through the curtains. Sister was standing in front of me.

'Congratulations!' she said.

'What?'

'It's a boy!'

I grinned like an idiot. I had a son.

'My wife?'

'She's fine. Mr Mallow sent me to give you the news. He'll tell you as soon as it's all right for you to go up.'

I think I cried with happiness, but when Mr Mallow came down, immaculate in spite of his night's work, I was composed; for the first time in twenty-four hours I was able to relax, and was feeling upset that Sylvia who had done all the work hadn't got the little girl she wanted.

Humphrey Mallow looked odd.

'Is everything all right?' A cold sweat of suspicion trickled down my back.

'Fine!' he said. 'But something rather strange has happened.'

I waited, hardly daring to think. The baby, Sylvia...

'There were two babies,' he said, looking at his nails.

I sat down, quite unable to speak.

'One must have been lying posteriorly. I never felt the second one at any time. They're both splendid. Not very large, but splendid. Incredible! Nothing's ever straightforward in doctors' families. They invariably do peculiar things.'

'The second one,' I said; 'is it a boy or a girl?'

'I really don't know,' Mallow said. 'I was too astounded to notice.'

'Excuse me.' Rudely, without even thanking him, I left him there.

On Sylvia's floor the babies in the nursery were crying for their early-morning feeds. A probationer carried a tray of feeding bottles down the corridor. A woman in labour called out.

Sister was closing softly the door of Sylvia's room. Beaming, she opened it to let me in.

Sylvia, still dopey from the anæsthetic she had received, watched me as I came near to the bed and into focus.

She held out her arms for me.

I hardly dared to ask.

'Darling,' I said, 'what was the second one?' I had only to look at the smile on her face to get the answer.

'Blonde?' I said.

She nodded.

'What about the pony-tail?'

'Give her time.'

We were too happy and for a while neither of us could speak.

'How is it that nobody knew?' Sylvia said a little later.

'That there were two babies?'

She nodded. 'I haven't got over the shock yet.'

'It's rare,' I said, 'but it happens. Sometimes one is lying posteriorly and it's not possible to feel it.'

'It seems too good to be true.'

'You're a very clever girl,' I said.

She was getting drowsy after her tiring night with no sleep.

'You'll have to get another cradle, Sweetie ... a laundry basket if you like ... I don't care ... and another set of vests and nighties ... Sweetie?'

'Yes.'

'Tessa Brindley's dead, isn't she?'

'Yes.'

'I knew you didn't want to upset me. But I guessed. You forget I love you.'

I knew she meant it. For the first time I was certain that I had worried unnecessarily about making her my wife, about tying her down to the wearing life of general practice.

She read my thoughts.

'I never could have been happy with Wilfred,' she said.

'No regrets?'

'No regrets. Don't tell anyone but it was rather boring being a model.'

'You'll have no time to be bored now.'

'I don't mind. I love it. The practice, the people asking my advice...' She was practically asleep.

'The phone?' I said.

'Who cares? I want to see my children.' She closed her eyes.

'I'll ask Sister,' I said, but by the time I got to the door she was fast asleep.

I sat down in the armchair and waited for her to wake up.

Humphrey Mallow came in to say goodbye.

The sunlight streamed over the blue blankets and washed the floor with light. The night staff went noisily off duty. The breakfast trolleys rattled down the corridor, and Sister sent in a tray of coffee and toast for me. The babies cried for their feeds and then were quiet again. The cleaner came in with her toothless grin and her clumsy broom.

It was midday when Sylvia woke. Together we looked at our son and daughter; minute, wrinkled and ugly, but the most wonderful babies I had ever seen.

Grinning inanely, I walked briskly along the rubber-floored corridor, tripped gaily down the stairs, whistled tunelessly through the hall and blinked out into the sunlight.

Opposite the hospital where a large notice said: 'No Parking. Ambulances Only,' George Leech was polishing a plum-coloured car.

'Congratcherlashuns, Doc!' he said, flicking an imaginary speck of dust from the mudguard.

'Thanks. Is this mine?'

'Asright. Ideal car for your job. I told you you'd have trouble with that other old iron.'

I walked round the car, inspecting it.

'George,' I said, 'there's something I've been telling *you* for long enough but you take no notice at all!'

He scratched his ear. 'Smatterofact,' he said, 'I changed me mind.' He jerked a thumb towards the hospital. 'P'r'aps I could go in now and book up for me op before I get second thoughts.'

'I shouldn't go in there if I were you,' I said. 'You might come out with a baby! I'll fix it up at St Anthony's for you.'

He held open the driving door. 'I'll be all right, won't I?'

'If you don't change your mind again. You don't want to be dead in a year, do you?'

'Nah,' he said. 'Me daughter's getting married. Sybil.'

I wondered if Sybil was aware that she had probably saved her father's life.

'I'll see to it straight away, George.' I turned on the ignition and the engine purred softly. 'Can I drive it home?'

'Natch.'

I pulled out into the sunlit side street. I had a new car, a new son and a daughter, a wife who loved me, and a life to save.

I was happy.

On the corner a raucous-voiced vendor was selling newspapers. I pulled up and he handed me one through the window.

'Wall Street Fall,' read the headlines. 'Shares Hit.'

A look inside confirmed my worst suspicions. I had hung on too long to my wonderful shares.

There was no chance that I would be retiring from general practice just yet.

But then, one can't have everything.

The publishers hope that this book has given you enjoyable reading. Large Print Books are especially designed to be as easy to see and hold as possible. If you wish a complete list of our books please ask at your local library or write directly to:

Dales Large Print Books
Magna House, Long Preston,
Skipton, North Yorkshire.
BD23 4ND

This Large Print Book, for people who cannot read normal print, is published under the auspices of

THE ULVERSCROFT FOUNDATION

... we hope you have enjoyed this book. Please think for a moment about those who have worse eyesight than you ... and are unable to even read or enjoy Large Print without great difficulty.

You can help them by sending a donation, large or small, to:

The Ulverscroft Foundation,
1, The Green, Bradgate Road,
Anstey, Leicestershire, LE7 7FU,
England.

or request a copy of our brochure for more details.

The Foundation will use all donations to assist those people who are visually impaired and need special attention with medical research, diagnosis and treatment.

Thank you very much for your help.